HOLY HELL

The tracker and the other rider were almost to the boulder. Suddenly both men straightened and gazed up past it.

Fargo glanced up, too, and was astounded to see Sister Angelina standing in plain sight, her hands calmly clasped in front of her, smiling her serene smile.

Terreros saw her, as well. "Get her!" he shouted, and the tracker and the other man tapped their spurs.

Fargo reared up. He had the Henry to his shoulder, the hammer already back. The tracker clawed for his revolver. The other man was a split instant slower. Fargo sighted and squeezed. The Henry boomed and the tracker was punched backward and sprawled in the dust. Instantly, Fargo sent a slug into the other bandit.

Fermin Terreros raised an arm and opened his mouth wide.

Centering the Henry's sights on the small man's chest, Fargo yelled, "Anyone moves and you die!"

THE TRAILSMAN

#349

NEW MEXICO GUN-DOWN

by

Jon Sharpe

A SIGNET BOOK

SIGNET
Published by New American Library, a division of
Penguin Group (USA) Inc., 375 Hudson Street,
New York, New York 10014, USA
Penguin Group (Canada), 90 Eglinton Avenue East, Suite 700, Toronto,
Ontario M4P 2Y3, Canada (a division of Pearson Penguin Canada Inc.)
Penguin Books Ltd., 80 Strand, London WC2R 0RL, England
Penguin Ireland, 25 St. Stephen's Green, Dublin 2,
Ireland (a division of Penguin Books Ltd.)
Penguin Group (Australia), 250 Camberwell Road, Camberwell, Victoria 3124,
Australia (a division of Pearson Australia Group Pty. Ltd.)
Penguin Books India Pvt. Ltd., 11 Community Centre, Panchsheel Park,
New Delhi - 110 017, India
Penguin Group (NZ), 67 Apollo Drive, Rosedale, North Shore 0632,
New Zealand (a division of Pearson New Zealand Ltd.)
Penguin Books (South Africa) (Pty.) Ltd., 24 Sturdee Avenue,
Rosebank, Johannesburg 2196, South Africa

Penguin Books Ltd., Registered Offices:
80 Strand, London WC2R 0RL, England

First published by Signet, an imprint of New American Library,
a division of Penguin Group (USA) Inc.

First Printing, November 2010
10 9 8 7 6 5 4 3 2 1

The first chapter of this book previously appeared in *Backwoods Brawl,* the three hundred forty-eighth volume in this series.

The Trailsman

Beginnings . . . they bend the tree and they mark the man. Skye Fargo was born when he was eighteen. Terror was his midwife, vengeance his first cry. Killing spawned Skye Fargo, ruthless, cold-blooded murder. Out of the acrid smoke of gunpowder still hanging in the air, he rose, cried out a promise never forgotten.

The Trailsman they began to call him all across the West: searcher, scout, hunter, the man who could see where others only looked, his skills for hire but not his soul, the man who lived each day to the fullest, yet trailed each tomorrow. Skye Fargo, the Trailsman, the seeker who could take the wildness of a land and the wanting of a woman and make them his own.

New Mexico, 1861—the Sangre de Cristo Mountains, where blood flows as freely as water.

1

A loud sound brought Skye Fargo out of the black pit of sleep. He sat up with a start. His first thought was that he had been shot. Pain exploded between his ears, and he winced and looked around in confusion. He was in a small room, lying on a bed, buck naked. The only other furniture was an old chest of drawers. A small, tattered rug lay near the door. So did five empty whiskey bottles.

"Hell," Fargo said. He seemed to recollect drinking a lot more than he should have, which explained the pain. His mouth felt as if it was stuffed with dry wool. When he swallowed, his throat felt raw.

From beside him came the loud sound: a snore that could shake walls.

Fargo glanced down at a shapely fanny and long velvet legs and it all came back to him in a burst of memory. The fanny belonged to a dove named Amalia. Last night they had sucked down bug juice until they were both in a stupor and come to her room for a frolic under the sheets. He didn't remember much about the frolic but it must have been a dandy, given how sore he was. He went to swat her backside but changed his mind. "Might as well let you sleep," he muttered.

Fargo swung his legs over the side and stood. The pounding grew worse. Smacking his dry lips, he shuffled around the bed. His buckskins and boots and gun belt were in an untidy heap. He recalled shedding them in a fit of passion and was annoyed that he hadn't kept his Colt handy. A mistake like that could cost him.

Fargo set to dressing. His body was stiff and he hurt all over, as if he'd been stomped by a bronc. He had bite marks

1

on his arms and his lower lip was swollen. He happened to see his reflection in a mirror over the chest of drawers. "Damn," he said. His neck bore a red mark the size of an apple and there were deep scratches on both shoulders. "You're a firebrand, woman," he said with a chuckle to the still-snoring Amalia.

It took a lot longer than it should have to put himself together. He was sluggish. He gave his head several hard shakes to try and clear it and regretted it when the pain became worse. Quietly opening the door, he slipped out. A window at the end of the hall was lit with the harsh glare of the New Mexico sun. His spurs jingling, he moved toward the stairs and was almost to them when someone came around the corner. They almost collided. He was looking down and all he saw was a pair of shoes and part of what he took to be a dress. "Watch where the hell you're going."

"I beg your pardon, young man."

Fargo raised his head. "Oh," he said, for lack of anything better.

It was a woman in her sixties, or older. She had more wrinkles than a prune but sparkling blue eyes and the sweetest smile this side of an angel, which was fitting since she wore a habit complete with a hood and baggy sleeves.

"I didn't mean to startle you," the nun said.

"You didn't," Fargo said more gruffly than he meant to. He went to go around her but she put a hand on his arm.

"I wonder if you could help me."

"Not now, ma'am." Fargo took a step but she held on to him.

"It's important. I'm looking for someone. Perhaps you know him."

"Lady, all I know is that I need a drink." Fargo smiled and shrugged loose and went down the stairs two at a stride. By the time he reached the bottom his head was hammering to rival a church bell. He crossed the lobby and walked out into the hot afternoon air. The bright light was so painful, he had to squint against the glare.

Las Emociones was a few doors down. Last night it had bustled with life and laughter but now only a handful of pa-

2

trons were at tables and the bar. He smacked to get the barkeep's attention. "Whiskey."

The bartender was portly and friendly and wore a white cotton shirt he somehow kept spotlessly clean. He brought a bottle and said, "More, senor? If I had as much as you, I would be drunk for a week."

A few chugs and the wool was gone from Fargo's mouth. He smiled and said, "*Gracias*. I needed that."

"Amalia?" the bartender said.

"Passed out and trying to bring down the hotel with her snores."

The man grinned. "She will be embarrassed, senor. She likes to boast that she can drink any man under the table. In you she has finally met her match."

"I think it was a tie but I woke up first." Fargo drank more red-eye and his body shook from the jolt. The pounding was going away and he could think again.

"Do you remember everything that happened last night?" the bartender asked.

"No," Fargo admitted.

"That is too bad, senor."

"Why?"

"Because there is about to be trouble." The bartender gazed toward the entrance and bobbed his chin.

Fargo turned.

Two men were coming toward him. Both had hard dark eyes. Both wore sombreros and pistols. They looked enough alike to be brothers. When they stopped, the taller, and probably the older, put his hands on his hips, his right hand inches from his six-shooter. "Did you think we would forget you, gringo?"

For the life of him, Fargo couldn't remember either one. "Should I?"

The tall one glowered. "You imagine you are funny, yes? You treat us with contempt and think we will swallow the insult."

"Mister, I have no idea what you're talking about." Fargo went to raise the bottle and the tall one struck his arm, nearly causing him to drop it.

3

"No more drink for you, gringo. You have us to deal with now."

Anger flushed through Fargo's veins. He set the bottle on the bar and lowered his arms. "Who the hell *are* you?"

"I am Juan Francisco de Salas and this is my brother, Jose. You will do us the honor of stepping into the street."

"Why would I want to do that?"

"What you want doesn't matter. It is what *we* want. We were not armed last night when you knocked me down but we are armed now. You will come with us out into the street and we will settle this as men should."

Fargo looked at the bartender. "I knocked him down?"

"*Sí*, senor. They come here often. Juan is fond of Amalia. He wanted her last night but she was with you. She refused to go with him. When he tried to take her you told him to . . ." The bartender scrunched up his face. "What was it you said? Ah, yes. Now I remember. You told him to 'go fuck himself.' Juan became upset and hit you. That was when you knocked him down and his brother had to carry him out."

Fargo smiled grimly. "Well, well, well."

"The cause of the insult is not the issue," Juan said. "Now will you come with us or not?"

"Not," Fargo said, and kneed him in the groin. Juan folded over with a grunt. Fargo launched an uppercut that raised Juan onto the heels of his boots and sent him tottering against a table. Both crashed to the floor. The brother, Jose, was rooted in disbelief. It enabled Fargo to take a quick step, streak out his Colt, and slam the barrel against Jose's temple. Both brothers were unconscious, Juan with blood trickling from his mouth, Jose with scarlet seeping from a gash in the side of his head. Fargo twirled the Colt into his holster. "Peckerwoods."

The bartender was agape. "*Caramba!* You are *rapido como el rayo*, senor. Quick as lightning."

Fargo grabbed the whiskey bottle. He slapped coins on the bar to pay for it and turned to go.

"A word, senor?" the bartender said.

Fargo stopped.

The bartender gestured at the forms on his floor. "They will not forget this. They will come after you."

"Tell them I said good luck finding me." Fargo intended to be well out of Santa Fe before the hour was up.

"They will find you, senor," the bartender said. "They are most persistent, the Salas brothers."

"It will be too bad for them if they do."

"No, senor. I am afraid it will be bad for you. They are rich, the Salas family. They have a large hacienda with many cattle and many vaqueros. Their father will not take kindly to what you have done. When he hears of it, he will send some of his vaqueros to track you down and restore the family's honor."

"Hell," Fargo said. All he'd wanted when he stopped for the night was a few drinks and a card game and a friendly dove to warm his lap.

"Or it could be the brothers will come after you themselves. It is a great insult, you beating them, and they must repay you or live in shame."

Fargo sighed.

"I only say this to warn you. I like you, senor. And it was not you who started the trouble last night."

"I'm obliged."

"What will you do?"

"Light a shuck, I reckon," Fargo said.

"Pardon, senor?"

"I don't want to kill them if I don't have to."

"If they find you, you will have to. Knocking you down would not be enough. *Comprendes*, senor?"

"*Comprendo*," Fargo said. To some folks, honor was worth dying over. He was about to turn and go when the bartender looked past him again and gave a slight start. Fargo spun, thinking it was more trouble.

It was the old nun. She was inside the batwings, her hands clasped at her waist, her features serene.

Everyone else stopped what they were doing to stare.

"Madre Superiora!" the bartender exclaimed, and rattled off a string of Spanish so fast, Fargo caught only half the words.

The nun came toward them, smiling. She saw the two brothers on the floor and her smile changed into a frown of disapproval. "Did you do this, senor?"

"They started it," Fargo said, and for some reason he flashed back to the time when he was eight or nine and his mother caught him and his brother fighting over an apple.

"You should not be in here, Mother Superior," the bartender said to her.

"Why not?"

The bartender gestured. "This is not the kind of place for a person like you."

"And what kind of person am I?" She touched her habit. "Under this I am just like you."

"No, you are not," the bartender said. "You are good. You are holy. This place is for the wicked."

"Oh, Carlos," she said.

The bartender blushed. "I am serious. You must leave."

"I can't," the nun said.

"Why not?"

"I must have words with him." She nodded at Fargo.

"Me?" Fargo wasn't sure he'd heard right.

"*Sí*, senor. Perhaps we could sit at a table and talk? It is very important. It is why I came to the hotel looking for you. But you walked off before I could explain."

"Please, Mother Superior," Carlos pleaded. "Not in here, I tell you. Go somewhere more fitting."

Juan Francisco de Salas groaned and his right hand twitched.

Fargo took that as a cue to touch his hat brim. "I'm sorry, ma'am. I have to fetch my horse and fan the breeze." He went around her and got out of there.

The livery was across the plaza. To the north of the city a high peak wore a crown of white despite it being early summer.

Fargo passed a man leading a burro and a woman carrying a large vase. No one paid attention to him. Ever since the war with Mexico and the Treaty of Guadalupe, *Norte Americanos*, as they were called, had been coming down the Santa Fe Trail in increasing numbers. Many liked the warm climate. Many liked the relaxed way of life. More than a few, notably those who lived outside the law, came to get away from the law's long reach.

The Ovaro was in the same stall where Fargo had left it. He threw on his saddle blanket and his saddle and slipped a bridle on and led the stallion out into the bright sunlight. He was raising his leg to hook his boot in the stirrup when the Salas brothers came out of the cantina. Each had a hand on his pistol. They looked about them, evidently searching, but he was on the off side of his horse and they didn't spot him. Juan said something to Jose and they moved around the edge of the plaza.

Fargo lowered his leg. Holding on to the reins, he turned in the other direction, keeping the stallion between them and him. They reached the north end as he reached the south. They turned to the west. He turned to the east. He was glad it wasn't siesta time or the plaza would be practically empty. As it was, there were enough people that he didn't stand out.

The Salas brothers reached the northwest corner. Fargo reached the southeast corner.

He could go down any of the narrow side streets but the one he wanted was near the cantina.

The brothers stopped and so did he. He watched them over the Ovaro's neck. They intently scanned the plaza, then they began to argue. Juan motioned one way and Jose the other. Finally they went the way Juan wanted and entered a side street and disappeared.

"Good riddance," Fargo said. He walked on and was almost to the cantina when the brothers came back out of the street and stood scouring passersby. Fargo swore and stopped. They were almost directly across from him. He was debating whether to climb on the stallion and use his spurs when the old nun stepped out of the cantina.

"There you are."

"Leave me be," Fargo said.

"I can't. It is too important."

"So is me getting shot."

"Ah. I see the brothers over there."

"Go away." Fargo motioned, shooing her, but she came over to the Ovaro.

"I intend to have my say."

Across the plaza, both brothers were making for the cantina.

"Oh, hell," Fargo said.

2

"I will help you if you will hear me out."

Fargo had no desire to spill blood. It might bring the law down on him and he didn't need that. "Help me how?"

"Stay behind your horse." The nun moved around to the other side and went a short way and stood waiting. When the brothers were near enough she raised a small hand and called out in Spanish, "Juan. Jose. Hold up a moment."

The brothers stopped but they did not look happy.

"What do you want?" Juan asked.

"Haven't you been in enough trouble for one day? What will your mother think? What will your father say?"

Juan flushed and said, "With all due respect, Mother Superior, this is none of your affair. Go bother someone else."

"Don't talk to her like that," Jose said.

The nun walked up to Juan. Her head came only as high as his chest yet she looked him in the eyes and poked him and said, "Your younger brother has more respect for the church than you do."

"Don't put words in my mouth."

"I have known you since you were in diapers, Juan Francisco de Salas. I have known your parents longer. I will go to them and I will tell them how you behave. I will tell Father Sebastian, too."

"Oh God," Juan said.

"You are too wild, too headstrong. Keep acting as you do and you will turn out like Fermin Terreros. Is that what you want?"

"I am not a *bandido*," Juan said resentfully.

"He was not always one, either. Then he took to drinking and fighting and being with loose women. Is that not what you do? To your shame, you are leading your poor brother down the same path." She sadly shook her head.

"You presume too much."

Jose gripped his brother's wrist. "Do not say such things, do you hear me? Not to her, of all people."

"Thank you, Jose," the old nun said.

Juan brushed his brother's hand off. "I will not stand here and be lectured to. I am a grown man and can do as I please." With that he wheeled and stalked off toward the south end of the plaza.

Jose lingered. "I am sorry, Mother Superior. He has always had a temper. But at heart he is a good man. Please do not speak ill of him to our mother and father or to Father Sebastian. It will only make him mad."

"For you, Jose, I will keep quiet. But if I do you a favor, you must do me one."

"Anything, Mother Superior."

"Keep a close eye on your brother. I was not exaggerating about Fermin Terreros. Your brother walks a path that can lead him to great trouble."

"I will watch over him. I promise."

"If you ever need my help . . ." The nun grasped the younger man's hand and warmly pumped it. "Go with God." She watched him hurry after Juan, then turned and came back around the Ovaro. "There. I have helped you. Now will you listen to what I have to say?"

"You're a tough old bird," Fargo said.

"When I need to be. I am Sister Angelina."

"I don't need to call you Mother Superior?" Fargo half joked.

"Are you of my faith?"

"No."

"Then Sister Angelina will do. I am also the Mother Superior at the Sisters of Apostolic Grace Convent, and it is in that capacity that I have sought you out."

"I don't savvy," Fargo said.

Sister Angelina smiled her sweet smile. "I want to hire you."

Fargo began to laugh but caught himself and cocked his head, studying her. "You're not joshing me?"

"I am in earnest, senor." She placed her small hand on his. "Please. I will only take a little of your time. If you refuse, so be it. But at least listen to my offer."

Fargo squinted up at the furnace in the sky. "Out here in the sun?"

"There is a *restaurante* around the corner. It is quiet and cool. We can sit there and have our talk."

Fargo's inclination was to say no. He'd had enough of Santa Fe to last him a spell. He could climb on the Ovaro and head for Texas and forget all about his hangover and the Salas brothers. But he heard himself say, "Lead the way."

The Armadillo, it was called, an adobe building with a low ceiling. The tables and chairs had seen a lot of use. A heavyset woman took their order. Fargo was famished and asked for a plate that consisted of three tacos, a burrito and pinto beans. Sister Angelina requested a glass of water and a bowl of soup.

"That's all?" Fargo said.

"I should not be a hog seeing as you are paying for it." She smiled her sweet smile and settled back in her chair. "Shall we get right to business?"

"You said something about hiring me." As best Fargo could recall, this would a first—hired by a nun, of all things.

"*Sí*. I am in need of a guide. Or maybe the right word would be escort. Someone like you. A scout. A man of the wilds. Someone who would be very much at home in the mountains." Sister Angelina folded her hands on the table. "I asked at Fort Marcy and the *coronel* says he knew just the man for the job. He said he is a friend of yours, and that he knew you were in town and staying at the hotel. So I went there looking for you. I am ashamed to say that when we bumped into one another, I did not realize who you were. The *coronel* had described you to me but you are much more handsome than I had reason to expect. You must be popular with the ladies."

"Are nuns supposed to notice things like that?"

"A handsome man is a handsome man. A pretty woman is a pretty woman." Sister Angelina spread her hands. "Do you not notice if a woman is appealing?"

"I'm too shy to look."

Sister Angelina covered her mouth and uttered a girlish giggle. "Senor, you are a terrible liar. I suspect all you do is look."

"Not all," Fargo said.

"It was never of much interest to me and is of no interest at all now that I am in my waning years. There will come a day when you, too, have no interest."

"When hell freezes over."

"Trust me, senor. You will not have the same urges at sixty as you do now. Our bodies change. We change. Believe it or not, there will come a day when you are not interested in women."

"I'll give them up for sheep?"

Sister Angelina's mouth dropped. She snorted, then covered her mouth again, and laughed. "You are terrible, senor. Do you know that?"

"The ladies reckon differently," Fargo said. "You don't believe me, we can go ask the one I left in the hotel room."

"Amalia," Sister Angelina said.

"You know her?"

"I know practically everyone in Santa Fe. Those of Spanish descent, anyway. It comes from living here all my life." She grew serious. "But let us talk more about your urges. Can you control them, Senor Fargo?"

"That's a mighty strange question."

"I have my reasons for asking."

"Control them how?" Fargo asked in amusement. "On a public street I can usually keep my britches on. Throw me in a room with a naked woman and my self-control flies out the window."

"How about deep in the mountains?"

Fargo sat back. "No more beating around the bush, Sister. What's this about?"

"It is about two young and pretty senoritas. They are sisters, from a poor family. Their father works at a stable. He feeds the horses, sweeps out the stalls, that sort of thing. Their mother stays at home and tends to their goats and chickens and their cow."

"What does all that have to do with me?"

"Patience, senor. The family's name is Vallejo. The older

daughter is Dalila. She loves life, that one. The younger is Paloma. Her names means 'dove.' She is kind and considerate and a fine young lady."

"Good for her," Fargo said.

"You are impatient with me. Very well. I will get to the point, as you *Norte Americanos* like to say." Sister Angelina gazed out the window. "The two are to become nuns. They are to travel to the Sisters of Apostolic Grace Convent to take their vows."

"Your convent."

"I am in charge, yes, but I would not call it mine. It is the Lord's. It is high up in the mountains. To get there takes nearly a week. There is no road but there is a trail."

"Why is it so far out?"

"It was built by the Spanish many years ago. They built many churches, too, as you must well know."

"I've seen a few."

"We are a cloistered community, senor. Like monks in a monastery. We are of the world but not in it. By staying apart, we stay pure. Do you understand?"

Fargo was about to say that he thought it was silly. Then he thought of how much he liked the wilds, and how for weeks at a time he would go off by his lonesome to get away from his so-called fellow man. "Maybe I do."

"Savage beasts roam the mountains, bears and wolves and whatnot. There are rattlesnakes and scorpions. There are Indians. Apaches, for instance. We have tried to make friends with them but they are wary of anyone who is not Apache. Then there are the *bandidos*, the bandits. They have little respect for our calling. Just last year Fermin Terreros and his men caught one of the younger members of our order outside the walls and did unspeakable things to her."

"They raped her?" Fargo guessed.

Sister Angelina sadly bowed her head, and nodded. "Yes," she said softly. "Not just one of the bandits or a few of them but all of them. When they tired of her they left her to die, but some prospectors found her and brought her back to us."

"She was lucky the bandits didn't kill her."

Sister Angelina looked up and her eyes were moist. "She has not spoken since. She sits in a chair all day and stares off

12

into space. We must feed her and wash her and clothe her. Once she was so lively and lovely. Now she is empty inside." She fell silent and a tear trickled down her cheek.

Fargo waited for her to go on. He had seen too much brutality to be shocked by her tale.

It was part and parcel of life on the frontier. If a person couldn't accept that, they should move back east where the worst they had to worry about was stubbing their toe.

Sister Angelina wiped her face with her sleeve, then smoothed her habit. She cleared her throat and said, "So as you can see, the trip is fraught with perils. Which is why I always make it alone."

"Are you loco?"

"Look at me, Senor Fargo," she said, and smiled. "Would anyone want to do to me as they did that poor sister? No. Would an Apache think it worth his time to slay someone so old? No. I can go back and forth with impunity."

"You take too much for granted."

"Perhaps I do. I also trust in the Lord and so far He has preserved me." She sobered. "But where I can travel safely, the Vallejo sisters cannot. If the bandits or the Apaches were to get hold of them, there is no telling what horrors those sweet girls would endure. To keep that from happening I must hire someone to escort us to the convent. To be our protector, if you will. That someone is you."

Fargo supposed he should be flattered but he was also puzzled. "Why didn't you ask the army to take you?"

"I could have, yes," Sister Angelina said. "The *coronel* would undoubtedly have been happy to help. But there are the Apaches to think of. Were they to see us with soldiers, it would anger them, and we have tried, as I have said, to be their friends."

She had a point, Fargo conceded. The Apaches hated the bluecoats, as they called the troopers. "But why *me*? There must be a hundred men in Santa Fe who could get you there safely."

"Most who live here are tradesmen or farmers. They are not Indian fighters. They have never had to deal with bandits. They barely know one end of a gun from the other."

Fargo grunted in assent. A lot of men on the frontier wore guns; few could shoot worth a damn.

"You, however, are a fighter. You have killed, the *coronel* told me. Only when you have had to, he says. You are not like Fermin Terreros, who kills for the perverse pleasure it brings him."

"I've had to blow out a few wicks," Fargo acknowledged.

"More than a few, I hear. He also says that you do not know the meaning of fear."

"Bullshit," Fargo bluntly responded. "I've been scared plenty of times."

"Yet that has not stopped you from living the life you do. You are at home in the wilds, where others are not. You are as good as an Indian at living off the land. You have the eyes of a hawk and the ears of a coyote."

"Hell," Fargo said. "You're laying it on a little thick."

"Pardon?"

"There's nothing special about me, Sister."

"I beg to differ. But be that as it may, you are the perfect man to take my charges and me to the convent. What do you say? A week of your time, if all goes well. Surely that is not too much of an imposition?"

"How much?" Fargo asked.

"Pardon?" she said again.

"You said you wanted to hire me. How much are you willing to pay me to get you there."

"I offer you my friendship."

Fargo blinked. "That's all?"

"It is all I have."

"You expect me to risk my hide against Apaches and bandits for *nothing*?"

"My friendship is hardly worthless, senor." Sister Angelina gave him another of her sweet smiles. "But yes."

"Son of a bitch," Skye Fargo said.

3

The Vallejo place was on the outskirts of Santa Fe. A total of eleven children plus the parents lived in a house no bigger than a shed. They shared it with chickens and three dogs and God knew how many cats. It sat on a two-acre plot. One of those acres was fenced and a cow and half a dozen goats were withering in the heat. A large vegetable garden was a testament to human optimism.

Fargo took it all in at a glance as he drew rein. Several barefoot children darted out of the house and stared as if they had never seen a gringo before. A big-boned woman, as wide as a buckboard, was hoeing in the garden. She stopped and put the hoe down and came over, mopping her sweaty brow.

Sister Angelina was on a mule nearly as old as she was. The only means of transportation the convent owned, she'd told Fargo. If anything ever happened to it, she didn't know how the nuns would get back and forth from Santa Fe. She slid off with the agility of a woman half her age and met the big-boned woman with a warm clasp and a hug. "Delores. It is wonderful to see you again."

Delores had eyes as big as her cow's, which she fixed on Fargo with suspicion. "Who is he and what is he doing here?"

"He is helping me take your lovely daughters to the convent," Sister Angelina said. "His name is Skye with an 'e.'"

"What sort of name is that for a man?" Delores asked. "They might as well have named him Earth or Water."

"Or Whiskey," Fargo said, and received a glance of reproach from Sister Angelina.

"You drink, do you?" Delores Vallejo said.

"Like a fish when I'm in the mood."

"Despicable," Delores said. "I do not. Nor my husband or my children. I do not permit it. Drink is the devil's poison."

"If that's the case I should be long dead."

Delores did not find it humorous. She turned to Sister Angelina. "You couldn't find anyone better than this, Mother Superior?"

"He is a scout, a frontiersman, as they are called. He will do fine."

"He is a wolf in buckskins," Delores said. "How can you expect me to let my daughters ride off with a man like him?"

"He has given his word he will behave."

"And you believe him? You are too trusting. You think everyone is good at heart, like you, when they are not." Delores gave Fargo a scathing scrutiny. "I would not trust him as far as I can throw his horse."

"I will be with them," Sister Angelina said.

"As you should be," Delores said. "But what could you do if he is not the good man you think he is?" She shook her head. "No, I will not permit my daughters to go until I am sure they can make the journey without harm."

Just then two more of her children came out of the house. To call them children, though, was an injustice. They were young women in the full bloom of life.

The older and taller had lustrous raven hair that cascaded in gentle swells to the small of her back. Her oval face was flawless, her top lip dimpled in the middle. Her eyes glittered with vitality and something else as she gazed up at Fargo in frank inspection. The plain yellow she wore did not seem so plain given the body it covered. Her breasts were ripe melons, her waist sapling thin. Her legs invited images of bedroom nights.

The younger woman was quite the contrast. Her hair was lighter, almost brunette. Her face was round, her cheeks full. She had a dreamy expression, as if she were thinking of things far away. She had nice proportions but her waist was too thick and her legs too short.

Fargo touched his hat brim to them and said, "How do you do?" He smiled at the tallest. "You must be Dalila." He smiled at the brunette. "And you must be Paloma."

"*Sí,*" Dalila said. She boldly walked over to the Ovaro and brazenly put a hand on his boot. Her smile was as dazzling as the sun. "*Caramba*," she playfully gushed. "Where did you come from? You are *magnifico*. Isn't he *magnifico*, sister?"

Paloma raised her dreamy gaze to Fargo. "He is just a man."

"Those broad shoulders, those blue eyes," Dalila said. "A girl could lose herself in them, I think."

Delores had her hands on her big hips and was glaring like a mad bull. Barreling over, she roughly pushed her oldest away from the stallion. "That will be enough out of you. Are you so man crazy that you must throw yourself at this gringo?"

"Oh, please," Dalila said sulkily. "All I did was greet him."

Delores poked Fargo's leg with a finger as thick as a spike. "I want you to leave, senor. I want you to leave this moment."

"*Un momento,*" Sister Angelina said. "If he goes, so do I. And if I go, your daughters stay here with you and you can forget about them joining our convent."

"What are you saying, Mother Superior?" Delores said.

"Didn't I make it clear? I have chosen this man to help escort your girls. I cannot take them alone. It is too dangerous. So either he comes or they don't go."

"But, Mother Superior . . ." Delores protested.

Sister Angelina held up a hand. "My mind is made up. Ever since you told me they were going to become nuns, I have been thinking hard about how to handle this."

"What is to handle?" Delores said. "I want them to go and they will go. It is as simple as that."

"I don't want to be a nun," Dalila broke in. "I have told you and told you, Mother, but you won't listen."

"It is my wish and my will and it is final," Delores declared. "Your sister and you are taking your vows."

Dalila folded her arms across her bosom and stamped her foot as if she were ten years old. "I hate it. You have no right."

"I'm your mother. I have all the right in the world."

"Wonderful," Fargo said. He reined away and went a few feet before Sister Angelina grabbed hold of a stirrup.

"Where are you going?"

"Texas."

"But our agreement?"

Fargo sighed and leaned on the saddle horn. "Lady, you've got your nerve. It's not bad enough you asked me to take lead or an arrow for you. Now I find out one of your would-be nuns doesn't want no part of it."

"Your heard their mother."

Fargo looked at Delores, who was glaring at Dalila. "Have her go with you. She's big enough to scare most anyone."

"Be serious, senor."

"This won't turn out well," he predicted.

"It will turn out exactly as I desire it should," Sister Angelina said. "Do you want to know why?" She slipped a hand under her habit at the throat and pulled out a long silver chain with a crucifix.

"Hell," Fargo said.

"Must you always swear so? Be patient with me, please. There is more to this than you can appreciate."

Fargo opened his mouth to flat out refuse and noticed Dalila admiring him, a long finger pressed to her dimpled upper lip. He did some admiring of his own; the swell of her large breasts, the sweep of her long thighs.

"You were about to say something?" Sister Angelina prompted.

"I should have been born a tree stump."

"Senor?"

"I'll take you and the ladies to the convent."

Sister Angelina squeezed his leg. "I can't thank you enough. You will be rewarded in the next life for the good deed you do for us."

Fargo almost snorted.

Delores was shooing Dalila and Paloma into the house to get ready to go. When they were inside she came back, her hard eyes fixed not on the Sister but on Fargo. "I still do not like this, Mother Superior. But if you say he must go, then I will accept your decision."

"He must," Sister Angelina said.

"He does look tough, doesn't he?" Delores said. "He has a hardness about him."

"If you only knew," Fargo said, more to himself than to them.

Delores grinned a wicked grin. "Do you know what he

reminds me of, Mother Superior, with that dark skin of his and his eyes like pieces of flint? A lizard."

"I went to Hawaii once on a ship," Fargo said. "There was this whale . . ." He would have gone on but Sister Angelina motioned for him to stop.

"You will not regret this, Delores. We need a protector and he is the best there is at this sort of thing."

"He is a gringo. You couldn't find one of our own to protect my beautiful girls?"

"Now, now," Sister Angelina said. "We must not judge others by the color of their skin. Do you want everyone to think you are a bigot?"

"I do not like gringos and I do not care if others know I do not like them. They are loud and have no manners and they treat us as if we are the dirt beneath their feet."

"Not all of them are that way."

Delores nodded at Fargo and made a loud sniffing sound. "And they smell different, too."

"Oh, Delores."

"We can't all of us be saints like you." Delores turned back to Fargo. "Listen to me, gringo, and listen good. If anything happens to my daughters, anything bad, I will have you hunted down and killed."

"Delores!" Sister Angelina exclaimed.

"I mean it, gringo. My children are everything to me. I love them dearly. They are why I slave as I do to try and give them a good life. Their future happiness is all that matters to me."

Fargo had had enough. "So you force two of them to become nuns whether they want to or not? You call that love?"

A red tinge spread from Delores's neck to her hairline. "How dare you? What do you know of having a family, gringo? What do you know of always doing the best for them even when they cannot see it is the best? Yes, I want Dalila and Paloma to be nuns. It is a great honor. I do not know how it is in your country but here nuns are held in great respect."

"This is my country," Fargo remarked. "Or did you forget this territory is part of the United States?"

"I forget nothing. I would rather we were still part of Mexico. You gringos come down here and you try to change us. You run around like ants, always busy, always trying to make more and more money, as if money is all that counts in this world."

Fargo had seen too much of it himself to argue. But he did say, "Not all of us are the same."

"Do not forget what I have told you. No harm must come to my girls. I trust Mother Superior's judgment, but I do not trust you."

"You can take your threat and shove it up your . . ." Fargo stiffened. Two of the boys were rolling a wooden hoop back and forth. They were near a corner of the house and hadn't noticed a snake coiled in its shadow. He saw the snake's head rise and heard the buzz of its tail.

Instantly, he drew and fired from the hip, fanning the Colt three times so swiftly the three shots sounded as one. The snake jumped into the air and fell, then commenced writhing in its death throes.

The boys were frozen in surprise.

Delores turned. "What were you shooting at? Was that to impress me with how quick you are?"

"No," Sister Angelina said. "Look here." She walked to the corner and pointed at the still-convulsing viper. "He saved your sons from being bitten."

Delores waddled over. She looked at the rattlesnake and at Fargo and at the snake again, and then she raised her foot and brought her heel down on its head and mashed the head into the dirt, grinding her shoe back and forth until the convulsions ceased. She smiled at Fargo. "Do you take my meaning, gringo?"

"Oh, Delores," Sister Angelina said.

Fargo began to reload. He could still light a shuck if he wanted, and he was considering just that when the girls came back out carrying bags. Dalila grinned and squared her shoulders so that her breasts pushed against her dress. He stopped thinking about lighting a shuck.

"You have everything you will need?" Sister Angelina asked them.

Paloma waggled her bag. "Mother had us pack last night. She said we must not keep you waiting when you came to take us."

"Do you resent becoming a nun as your sister does?" Sister Angelina asked.

"Not at all," Paloma said. "I very much look forward to devoting my life to the Lord. To being pure and holy like you." She gave her mother a radiant look. "And I will owe it all to my *madre*, who loves us with all her heart."

"I need a drink," Fargo said, but no one paid him any mind.

"We only have the mule and the horse," Sister Angelina was saying, "so we must ride double. One of you must ride with me and the other must ride with Senor Fargo."

Dalila eagerly stepped toward the Ovaro but stopped when her mother sharply said her name.

"You will ride with the Mother Superior. Paloma will ride with the gringo."

Fargo twirled the Colt into his holster with a flourish just to show off and then bent and offered his hand. "Here you go, little lady." Paloma took firm hold and he swung her up behind him. She was careful not to let her body touch his any more than was necessary.

"*Gracias*, senor."

Fargo took her bag and hung it from the saddle horn. It barely weighed anything. "What's in here? Feathers?"

"All that I own, senor."

Sister Angelina was slow climbing onto her mule. She held her hand down to Dalila but Dalila swung lithely on without any help.

"Go with God, all of you," Delores said. Her eyes misted and she clasped her hands under her chin. "This is the happiest day of my life."

"You are welcome to visit the convent any time to see them," Sister Angelina said.

Delores stabbed a finger at Fargo. "Remember what I said, gringo."

Fargo reined around and gigged the Ovaro. The promise of Dalila's ripe young body notwithstanding, he wasn't in the best of moods.

"Take care, Mother!" Paloma called back. "Don't worry about us. We will be fine." She let out a contented sigh and said, "This will be great fun, don't you think, Senor Fargo?"

"Like eating glass," Fargo said.

4

The Spanish and Fargo had something in common; they liked to wander, to explore. Fargo did it because he liked to see what was over the next horizon. The Spanish did it for conquest, and for gold, and to those ends they had penetrated deeper into the rugged fastness of the mountains in the Southwest than most anyone. They left plenty of signs they had been there: rock carvings, abandoned mines, deserted missions.

The Sisters of Apostolic Grace Convent was another of their legacies. Built in 1682, it had stood the twin tests of wear and time. When the Spanish relinquished control of the territory and many of their missions closed, the sisters at the convent refused to leave. They were devoted to their order, and to the poor. They performed many charitable works in Santa Fe and elsewhere. All across the territory they were held in the highest esteem.

All of which Fargo learned in the first couple of hours from Sister Angelina. He humored her and let her drone on while he stayed alert for trouble. Not that he expected any when they were only a few hours out of Santa Fe.

To the north reared Truchas Peak. Fargo had heard that it was over thirteen thousand feet high. Santa Fe itself sat at an elevation of seven thousand, making it higher than Denver, the mile-high city.

Truchas Peak was part of the formidable Sangre de Cristo range. The name meant Blood of Christ. Fargo figured it came from the red color of the peaks at sunset. The name was recent. The Spanish had called the range La Sierra. It was as remote as anywhere on the continent and still largely unexplored. Apache bands roamed with impunity. The Sangre de Cristos were also a haven for outlaws.

Back when the Spanish built the convent, the "natives" had been subjugated, or so the Spanish thought, and bandits were few. So long as the nuns stayed within their high walls, they were safe. Now it was different.

Fargo was curious. At one point he turned to Sister Angelina, who was riding beside him, and asked, "Why do you and the other sisters stay up in the mountains where it's so dangerous when you'd be better off down here?"

"Abandon our convent? We wouldn't think of it."

"You could have another built closer to Santa Fe," Fargo suggested.

"True," Sister Angelina agreed. "But what would that say about our faith if we let a few paltry dangers scare us off?"

"There's nothing paltry about the Jicarillas or the Mescaleros. If they wanted to, they could wipe you out without half trying."

"True again," Sister Angelina said. "That they have left us alone shows they think more highly of us than they do most of our kind."

Fargo knew the Apaches well. "Or they have too much pride to wage war on women."

"That too," Sister Angelina said. "In any event, we treat them no differently than we treat anyone else. We have given them food when the winters have been hard and have treated a few of their sick."

"Do you give the bandits food, too?"

"No. The banditos are a plague. They rob and hurt and kill as they please and no one can do anything to stop them. Not the sheriff, not the soldiers, not anyone."

"Can't blame the law or the soldiers," Fargo said. "The bandits have a million square miles to hide in." He was exaggerating but not by much.

The sisters had been quiet, listening, but now Dalila put a warm hand on Fargo's shoulder and said, "Someone is following us, senor." She had switched places with her sister when they stopped a while back so Sister Angelina could tighten her cinch on the mule.

Fargo drew rein and twisted in the saddle. The road to the mountains wasn't heavily traveled. They hadn't seen another rider in half an hour. But only a hundred yards back was a heavyset man on a dun. It bothered Fargo that the man had got so close without him noticing. He put his hand on his Colt.

"Surely there is no need for your weapon?" Sister Angelina said. "You can't shoot every traveler we see."

"He could be a bandit for all you know."

"Him?" Sister Angelina said, and laughed.

Fargo doubted it, too. The man rode with all the grace of a lump of mud. His arms kept flapping and his legs stuck out from the sides. As he drew nearer, Fargo saw that his rotund body jiggled like so much pudding. The man wore a dusty bowler and a suit fit to burst at the seams and didn't have a six-gun around his waist or a saddle scabbard with a rifle.

"Greetings, greetings," the man said enthusiastically. "I was hoping you would stop so I could catch up."

"Is that a fact?" Fargo said.

The man dipped his triple chins while removing his bowler. "Indeed it is. I hate to ride alone. I'd much rather have company."

Sister Angelina asked, "Where are you bound, sir, if I might ask?"

"Ask away," the man said cheerfully. "My name is Thaddeus J. Brewster, by the way. I sell ladies' apparel."

"Figures," Fargo said.

"I have just concluded a profitable stay in Santa Fe and I'm on my way to Trinidad," Brewster informed them.

"A far piece," Fargo observed.

"Indeed it is. All the more reason I would appreciate riding with you a spell. It gets lonely out in the middle of nowhere."

"You would be better off taking a stagecoach," Sister Angelina said.

"Probably. But stages cost money and I'm frugal." Brewster pulled a handkerchief from an inside pocket and dabbed at his sweaty moon face. "It sure is hot, isn't it? You'd almost think we were in the desert."

"We don't want your company," Fargo said.

Both the drummer and the Mother Superior said, "What?" at the same time.

"You heard me. We're keeping to ourselves."

"That's uncivilized," Brewster objected. "What harm can it do? You can see I'm as friendly as can be."

"A wolf can act friendly, too, until it bites you."

"Ridiculous," Brewster huffed. "Do I look like a wolf to you?"

"More like a toad," Fargo said.

Sister Angelina clucked to her mule and reined it around to the drummer's dun. "Pay no attention to him, Senor Brewster. He has a mean tongue. You are perfectly welcome to ride with us for as long as you'd like."

"I'm grateful, ma'am," Brewster said, and flashed Fargo a grin of triumph.

Fargo tapped his spurs. He was simmering. He needed to have a long talk with the nun but it could wait until they stopped for the night. He felt a slight shaking of the saddle and realized Dalila was quietly laughing. "Something strike you as funny?"

"You do. You act so big and tough but you let an old lady tell you what to do."

"Should you be talking about a nun like that?"

"I like her, but I don't want to join her order. I would rather die than spend the rest of my life in a convent."

"I gathered it was your mother's notion," Fargo said.

"You gather correctly. My mother has always said how wonderful it would be if her daughters became nuns. A lot of mothers say things like that, and I didn't think she was serious." Dalila paused. "But she was, and I hate her for it."

"You hate your own mother?"

"We have argued and argued and I cannot make her understand I do *not* want to do this. But she refuses to listen. She is deeply religious, and to her, this is her most dearly held dream come true."

"You're a grown-up," Fargo said. "You can make up your own mind."

"That is not how things are done here. Daughters are expected to obey. Always."

Sadness entered Dalila's voice. "I am trapped, senor. I will spend the rest of my life cloistered in a convent and hate every minute of it."

"You're only trapped if you let yourself be."

"I knew you would not understand. Our customs are different than yours. I wish with all my heart and soul that I could tell my mother no but I can't."

On that note she fell quiet.

Fargo concentrated on the terrain. It was mostly open until they reached the hills that served as stepping-stones to the mountains. Up there was where the bandits were, and the Apaches, and a host of other dangers. He glanced back at Thaddeus Brewster, who was amiably chatting with Sister Angelina. It bothered him that the man claimed to be riding all the way to Trinidad alone. A person had to be awful money hungry, or awful stupid, to risk their hide just to save a few dollars on stage fare.

The road gradually climbed. Patches of grama grass and mesquite and cactus became less common and pinion and scrub oaks more so.

It was pushing dark when they came to where the road bore to the northeast, and Trinidad. Fargo would have preferred to be shed of Brewster then and there and push on up the trail but Sister Angelina announced that she was weary and this was as good a spot as any for them to stop for the night. She took Dalila and Paloma to gather firewood while Fargo stripped the Ovaro and the mule.

Brewster was doing the same with his dun. "I guess we'll part company in the morning," he said.

Fargo grunted.

"That nun sure is a hoot. Feisty old girl, don't you think?"

Fargo grunted again.

"Don't talk much, do you?"

"When I have something to say."

"The quiet kind, huh? I bet the ladies love you." Brewster chuckled. "Me, I have to work at it. I either dazzle them with my smile and my charm or I get them so drunk they don't know what they're doing." He laughed too loudly. "Or I pay for it."

Fargo went back to grunting. Sometimes people took that as a hint.

"Those sisters sure are lookers, aren't they? Especially that one you're riding with. What's her name again, Dalila?"

"They're on their way to become nuns."

"So the sister told me. But that Dalila. What I wouldn't give to poke her. I bet she'd be a wildcat."

Fargo turned and put his hand on his Colt. "You'll never find out."

About to take off his saddle, Brewster thrust both hands out and shook his head. "No, no. Don't misunderstand. I'd never try anything. I'm not the kind. I was only saying, is all."

"Keep it that way."

"Damn, you're prickly. Are you supposed to protect their virtue as well as get them to that convent?" Brewster chortled to show it was a joke.

Fargo didn't find it funny. He went about spreading his blankets and propping his saddle and then filled the coffeepot from the waterskin he had brought. It should be enough to last them if they were careful about how much they used.

Sister Angelina and her charges returned, their arms laden with broken branches. They deposited them in a pile and Fargo kindled a fire and put the coffee on. For supper he cooked beans. It wasn't much but he was used to it.

Dalila wasn't. She sat with her arms around her chest and her knees drawn up, gloomily regarding the crackling flames. "Is that all we're having?"

"I'll shoot something tomorrow," Fargo said. A rabbit, a deer, anything would do.

"I am not fond of those kinds of beans."

Brewster opened his saddlebags and brought out a can. "How do you feel about peaches, little lady?"

Dalila brightened. "Those I like."

"Figured you might." Brewster rose and came around the fire and gave the can to her. "Here you go. Just for you. The sweetest, tastiest peaches this side of anywhere. I don't normally share them but in your case I'll make an exception."

"Thank you, senor. It is most kind of you."

"That's me," Brewster said. "Kind as can be."

"It is very gracious," Sister Angelina said. "Isn't it gracious of him, Senor Fargo?"

"Gracious as hell," Fargo said.

Brewster sat back down. The whole meal, he stared at

Dalila except when Fargo looked at him and then he would glance away. When it came time for the peaches he slurped his and smacked his lips a lot. "Delicious, aren't they?"

"Very," Paloma said. "We do not often get to eat them. We are a poor family."

Brewster didn't reply. Instead he said to her sister, "Pretty ladies like you should eat peaches every day and wear fine dresses and ride in a fancy carriage."

"That would be wonderful," Dalila said longingly. "But it will never happen, I am afraid."

"You never know," Brewster said.

"But I do, senor. I used to dream that the son of a rich hacienda owner would take an interest in me. We would marry and I would have all the fine things in life. But now I am to be a nun, and nuns cannot afford peaches."

"We eat well at the convent," Sister Angelina said. "Our fare is simple but we never go hungry."

"I would give my woman peaches every day if she wanted them," Brewster said with a meaningful look at Dalila.

"Damned generous," Fargo said, but the man ignored him.

"How is it you don't have a wife?" Sister Angelina asked.

Brewster shrugged. "I travel a lot. Most women want their husbands home more than I would be."

"What do you do for companionship?"

"That's sort of personal, isn't it?"

"Yes. Forget I asked."

Brewster gazed over his coffee cup at Dalila.

The women were tired and turned in early. Shortly after, Brewster stretched and yawned and announced, "I need to head out early so I should get some sleep, too." He lay down and in a while he commenced to snore.

Fargo sipped coffee and listened to the cries of coyotes and the far off howls of wolves. The predators were abroad. He let the fire burn low before he eased onto his back with his saddle for a pillow. Palming his Colt, he pulled his blanket up to hide it.

As surely as the sun rose and set, he knew what was going to happen.

5

Brewster probably thought he was clever or it took him a while to get up the nerve. By Fargo's reckoning midnight had come and long gone when the snoring stopped and Brewster slowly sat up. He looked at Fargo. Fargo let out a snore of his own and it must have been convincing. From under his hat brim he saw Brewster quietly rise and turn toward the women. Sister Angelina was a dozen feet or so from the others. Brewster stared at her as if to assure himself she was asleep and then he crept toward Dalila and Paloma. Dalila was curled on her side with her blanket to her chin. Paloma had her blanket pulled over her head against the night chill.

The fire had long since died. In the starlight something metallic gleamed in Brewster's hand. He went past Paloma and stood over Dalila. He looked again at the rest of them, then sank to a knee and suddenly pressed what he was holding to Dalila's throat and clamped his other hand over her mouth. She awoke with a start and made a slight sound but he whispered and she became still.

Brewster pulled her to her feet. Even in the dark, Fargo could see her eyes were wide with fear. Brewster moved toward the oaks, the blade still to her throat, his other arm around her waist. She was too frightened to struggle or call out. Both girls had gone to sleep fully dressed except for their shoes, and Dalila jerked her feet as if the ground hurt.

Fargo lay still and uttered another snore. The moment they disappeared he rolled up into a crouch, and circled. He figured Brewster would be intent on Dalila. He moved silently and cautiously once he was in the vegetation. All it would take was for a twig to snap to give him away. He looked but didn't see them. Concerned, he went faster. Brewster would take her far enough that they wouldn't be heard. He threaded through slender boles and there Dalila was, on her knees, her face in her hands, quietly weeping.

Brewster was nowhere to be seen.

Fargo took another step and the undergrowth exploded. He tried to spin but a shoulder rammed into him and he was lifted off his feet and sent tottering. He collided with an oak and shifted to take aim. A vise clamped onto his wrist. Steel sliced at his face. He caught hold of Brewster's wrist and they were face-to-face, Brewster wheezing like he had run ten miles.

"You won't stop me!" he growled.

Fargo drove his forehead against Brewster's nose. There was a *crunch* and the splatter of wet drops. His hat fell off. Brewster bleated in pain. The pain changed to fury and he slammed Fargo against a tree. Not all of Brewster's bulk was fat. A lot was muscle. The tip of the knife inched toward Fargo's neck.

Brewster's dark eyes glinted with his craving to kill. Rivulets ran from his nose over his mouth and chin.

Fargo hooked a boot behind Brewster's thick leg, and pushed. Brewster swayed but stayed on his feet. Fargo arced his knee at Brewster's groin. Brewster shifted and took the blow on his leg.

"Didn't think I'd be so tough, did you?"

Fargo smashed his forehead against Brewster's mouth. Brewster swore and pulled his head back so Fargo's couldn't do it again, which was exactly what Fargo wanted. He tucked his chin to his chest, then drove his head up and out and connected with the underside of Brewster's jaw. It hurt like hell but it also caused Brewster's knees to sag and his grip to weaken. Fargo wrenched his right arm free and clubbed Brewster on the temple. Brewster's knees sagged more but he still held on to the knife. Fargo slashed the Colt across Brewster's elbow. Brewster yelped and the knife fell.

"Damn you!"

A last slam of the Colt against Brewster's face and he pitched heavily onto his big belly and lay gasping and swearing.

Fargo kicked him in the head. That did it. The man was still.

Dalila had stopped crying and was gaping in amazement. *"Madre de Dios!"* she breathlessly exclaimed. "You were *magnifico*."

Fargo didn't feel so magnificent. His back was sore and his wrist ached and he was mad enough to put a slug into Brewster's brainpan. "Are you all right?"

"Sí."

Fargo helped her to stand and she leaned on him for support, her breasts against his chest. She was grinning. "You recover quick," he said. "A minute ago you were scared to death."

"I was crying because I did not want it to be him."

"Him what?"

"He said he was going to have his way with me and if I yelled he would slit my throat." Dalila put a hand to Fargo's cheek. "But I am safe now. You came and you rescued me."

Brewster groaned.

Fargo retrieved his hat. He turned, holstered the Colt, and grabbed the back of Brewster's jacket and dragged him. He didn't care that Brewster bumped over rocks and against trees and had to be hauled over a log.

Dalila pranced at his side like a schoolgirl on a lark. "What will you do, senor? Kill him, I hope."

"No."

"Didn't you hear me? He said he would do terrible things to me. I think you should shoot him. Or perhaps hang him."

"If I had an ax I could chop him into bits and pieces."

"You would do that for me?"

"Hell." Fargo hauled Brewster's stirring form to the embers of their fire. He poked at them with a stick and uncovered a few that glowed red. It only took a minute and flames licked at the sky. He planted his boot in Brewster's ribs. "Sit up, you son of a bitch. I know you're faking."

Brewster's eyes snapped open. They were mirrors of hate. His hand to his side, he slowly obeyed. "I won't forget this."

Fargo kicked him in the shoulder and Brewster sprawled onto his back. "Don't talk unless I say you can."

"Bastard."

Fargo kicked him in the groin. Brewster doubled, clutching himself, and mewed in agony. Bending, Fargo patted him to see if he carried hideouts. In a pocket he found a three-barreled pocket pistol and in another pocket a knuckle-duster. He tossed both onto his blankets.

Sister Angelina had sat up and was looking about in confusion. "What is going on? What are you doing up, Dalila? And what is wrong with Senor Brewster?"

Dalila was watching Fargo in rapt fascination. "Senor Brewster is a pig. He was intent on ravishing me but Senor Fargo stopped him." She said Fargo's name as if she were caressing it. Or him.

For a woman of her years, Sister Angelina was remarkably spry. She practically bounded to her feet. "Can this be?"

"I warned you but you wouldn't listen," Fargo said.

"How was I to know?" Sister Angelina replied. "He seemed like such a nice man. He gave us no cause to suspect him."

"We shouldn't trust anyone until you're safe behind the walls of your convent."

Sister Angelina solicitously placed her hand on Brewster. "Are you in a lot of pain, senor?"

"Of course I'm in pain, you stupid cow," he gurgled. "The son of a bitch kicked me in the balls."

"My goodness. Is there anything I can do?"

Brewster raised his head. Spittle flecked his lips and his chin was dark with blood. "You can drop dead, bitch."

Fargo picked up the knuckle-duster. He slid his fingers through the holes and closed his fist. Brewster was glowering at Angelina and didn't see him turn or cock his arm. He unleashed a right cross that ruptured flesh and left Brewster in a heap.

"Senor!" the nun cried. "Please! There has been enough violence."

"I'm just getting started." Fargo went to his saddle and got his rope. He wrapped an end several times around Brewster's ankles and looped the rope several times around Brewster's wrists, then tied it tight around Brester's neck so that if Brewster struggled he would choke.

"Is that necessary?" Sister Angelina asked.

"We don't tie him, he's liable to bash our heads in while we sleep."

"Surely you are exaggerating."

Fargo knelt on his blankets and picked up the three-barreled pocket pistol. They weren't all that common. As best he recollected, this model was made by a company called Marston. He shoved it into his saddlebag and stretched out on his back.

"You're not going to question him? Ask him why he behaved so abominably?"

"I know why."

"Enlighten me," Sister Angelina requested.

"He likes to rape women." Fargo pulled his hat low. There were four hours or so until daylight and he could use the sleep.

"I do not approve of your behavior, senor. What he did was despicable but we shouldn't leave him tied there like"—Sister Angelina couldn't seem to find the right words—"like some sort of rabid dog."

"He stays tied until I say different."

"Can't we talk about this?"

"No."

"This is not a good start to our journey," Sister Angelina said.

"No," Fargo said. "It's not."

Fortunately, she let it drop and went to her blankets. Dalila, though, came over and placed her hand on his arm.

"Thank you, senor, for saving me."

"De nada."

"You are my hero."

"Go to sleep." Fargo rolled over and heard her move off. He listened to the rustle of her dress and her blankets and when it was quiet he raised his head be make certain she had turned in.

Paloma was propped on her elbows, staring at him.

Fargo suspected she had been awake the whole time. He smiled but she didn't return it. Strange girl, he thought, and settled down. It took a while to drift off but at last he did, only to sleep uneasily and snap awake at every slight noise.

The squawk of a jay woke him as a pink flush was spreading across the eastern horizon. Fargo sat up and stretched. His back still hurt some from where Brewster had slammed him against the tree. That reminded him. He shifted. "Been up long?"

Brewster was staring at him with the same hate-filled eyes as last night. "You tie damn tight knots."

"I try." Fargo stood and breathed deep of the crisp morning air. Mornings had long been one of his favorite times of the day.

"Untie me."

"When I'm good and ready." Fargo stepped to the embers. Once more he kindled a flame to life and puffed to keep it going. He gave the coffeepot a shake. Fully half was left. "Good," he said. He wouldn't need to make more since the nun and the girls didn't drink it.

"How about taking this rope off my neck," Brewster requested. "It's about scraped me raw."

"Tough."

Fargo made biscuits, one for each of them except Brewster. It wasn't much but they didn't have a packhorse and the few supplies he'd brought had to last. The aroma woke Sister Angelina, who rose smiling. It died when she set eyes on Brewster.

"Oh. I almost forgot." She adjusted her habit and came to the fire. "*Buenos días*, Senor Fargo."

"Morning." Fargo slid the biscuits from the pan onto a tin plate and set them aside to cool.

"How long must we keep Senor Brewster tied up? It is inhumane."

"We should talk about that," Fargo said. "The way I see it, we have three choices."

"What are they?"

"We can shoot him."

Sister Angelina made a *tsk-tsk* sound. "That is a terrible joke. You have a vicious streak, I think."

"Who's joking?" Fargo said. "He tried to rape Dalila. Who knows how many other women he's done it to? We let him go, he'll go on doing it. Or he might follow us and jump us when our guard is down."

"You could stop him. You stopped him last night."

"Barely."

"Well, killing him is still not an option. It would be cruel of us to take his life when he is helpless. I will not condone killing except in the most extreme circumstances."

"The second choice is to throw him over his dun and take him back to Santa Fe and turn him over to the law."

"And lose a full day? I would not like that."

"Didn't reckon you would," Fargo said. "So that leaves setting him free and sending him on his way."

"I pick that one," Sister Angelina said.

"Me too," Brewster said.

"You don't have a say." To the nun Fargo said, "Wake the girls and we'll eat and be on our way."

Paloma was her usual quiet self. She accepted her biscuit without saying thanks and hardly looked at Brewster.

Dalila took longer to rise. She was slow getting up and slow moving to the fire and just as slow smearing butter on her biscuit and chewing. She did look at Brewster. Then she said, "Pig."

"You wanted it and you know it."

Fargo casually got up and casually stepped over and brought the heel of his boot down hard on Brewster's stomach. Brewster howled and thrashed wildly. "The next time it's your teeth."

Sister Angelina was horror-struck. "That was terrible. You are not at all as nice as the *coronel* said you were."

"There's something you better understand. When I take a job I don't do it halfway. I do whatever needs doing to get it done."

"Are you saying you might do this to someone else?"

"I'm saying," Fargo said with infinite patience, "that before we reach this convent of yours, a lot worse could happen."

6

The bright glare of the rising sun splashed the countryside. The man called Brewster stood in the middle of the road glaring at Fargo, on the Ovaro. Fargo's hand was on his Colt.

"Get going."

"You never said anything about taking my horse."

Fargo shrugged. "Think of it as your good deed for the year. The Sisters of Apostolic Grace thank you."

"It's stealing," Brewster angrily declared, "and they hang horse thieves in this part of the country."

"They hang bastards who try to rape women, too." Fargo nodded in the general direction of Santa Fe. "On your way."

Brewster appealed to Sister Angelina. "How about you? Are you going to let him do this to me? You're supposed to be a woman of God, for God's sake."

"When was the last time you were in church?" she asked.

"What?"

"You heard me, Senor Brewster. When was the last time you attended services? Recently, perhaps?"

"Hell, no. Not since I was a kid. My mother always made me go on Sunday and I hated it."

"Have a nice walk," Sister Angelina said.

Brewster stared at the sisters Dalila and Paloma mounted double on his horse. "Don't you let anything happen to him, you hear? I'll be coming for him one of these days."

"Walk," Fargo said.

Brewster turned and tramped down the road, an over-dressed toad who would stop in a while and wait for dark when it was cooler. Fargo reckoned it would take him two to three days to reach Santa Fe, and by then they would be well into the mountains. He reined the Ovaro around and headed up the trail that would take them into the heart of the Sangre de Cristos. It was wide enough for two horses to ride abreast so he wasn't surprised when the stallion acquired a mule shadow.

"You have something to say, say it."

"You have me at odds with myself," Sister Angelina said. "Part of me is appalled at what you did."

"And the other part?"

She grinned. "The other part believes he got what he deserved."

"No, what he *deserved* was a trial and a necktie social," Fargo said. "Or a bullet. But you didn't want me to do that."

"You are a hard man, senor."

"It's a hard life."

"Yet here you are, helping me take the senoritas to the convent. Maybe you are not as hard as you pretend to be."

"I won't be pestered the whole way," Fargo said.

"Is that what I am doing? I thought I was complimenting you." Sister Angelina chuckled and fell back to ride next to her charges.

To Fargo, there was a simple explanation for him agreeing to help her: He was a lunkhead. He should have told her to take a leap off a cliff. He almost did, until he set eyes on Dalila. All it took was a pretty face and a nice pair of thighs, and he was like a buck in rut. He couldn't get enough. With other men it was liquor or cards. With him it had always been women. "Damn females," he muttered. But he wasn't fooling himself. It was his craving for them that got him into trouble, not the women themselves.

Beyond the hills the trail climbed steeply, winding like an earthen snake. The mountains reared stark and formidable, ancient ramparts reaching to the clouds. The Sangre de Cristos lived up their name; when the sun was right, the upper slopes were bloodred.

Some people, Fargo reflected, would take that as an omen.

They saw no one else all the rest of the day. Few were intrepid enough to dare the haunts of the Apaches and roving bandit bands. Even the cavalry rarely penetrated this far in.

Fargo rode with every sense alert, his hand nearly always on his Colt.

Sister Angelina, on the other hand, acted as if she didn't have a care in the world. She smiled and chatted with the Vallejo sisters. One moment she was enthralled by a high-flying eagle and the next by a scampering squirrel. Toward the middle of the afternoon a snake slithered across the trail and she squealed in delight.

"Oh look! Did you see that?"

"Another damned rattler," Fargo said. He would have shot it if it had coiled to strike at the horses.

"I'm beginning to suspect you do not appreciate the great diversity of life," Sister Angelina said.

"A snake is a snake," Fargo said. "Don't make more of it than there is."

"But that is my point, senor. All forms of life are a gift from our Creator, given to us that we might enjoy them."

"Don't start." Fargo would take them to the convent but he wouldn't be preached to.

"You are touchy on this subject."

"I'm touchy about people telling me what to think," Fargo clarified. "You see things your way. I see them mine. Let's leave it at that."

"I see them God's way."

Fargo shifted in the saddle and stared at her.

"Oh, very well." Sister Angelina's face lit with amusement. "I will behave. But it will be hard."

"I'm obliged."

An hour before sundown a rabbit did the same as the snake. It made the mistake of pausing to look at them and twitch its long ears, and Fargo snapped a shot from the hip that cored its head. After they made camp he skinned it and rigged a spit and speared dripping pieces of meat with a sharp stick.

"I'm hungry enough to eat a cow," Dalila remarked. She was seated on her blanket, her sister a few feet away on hers.

"You always eat like a bird," Paloma said, "so you won't lose your figure."

Sister Angelina was lying on her side, resting. She propped her head on her hand and said, "Once you put on one of these"—she touched her habit—"how you look will no longer matter."

"It will to me," Dalila said.

"You are young yet. But you will change. You will come to realize that the spirit is important, not the flesh."

"You sound like my mother. She's the one who should have been a nun."

Sister Angelina laid her head back down. "God works in mysterious ways."

Fargo hoped they didn't bicker the whole way. He'd put a stop to it quick. He touched the coffeepot but it wasn't hot enough yet. Settling back, he scanned the miles-high peaks with their phalanxes of timber and treacherous talus. The sun was gone and dark was descending.

"May I ask you a question, senor?" Paloma said.

Fargo was surprised. She hardly ever spoke to him. "Sure."

"Are all gringos like you? We have not met many of your kind. My mother says you are animals."

"Paloma!" Sister Angelina declared.

"Well, she does." To Fargo Paloma said, "You are the first gringo I have gotten to know. So I ask you again, are all gringos like you?"

"Are all of your people the same?"

"No, of course not."

"Then don't ask stupid questions." Fargo turned the stick so the meat roasted evenly. The delicious smell made his stomach rumble.

"I thought as much but I wanted to be sure."

Fargo scanned the mountains again and a tingle ran down his spine. He sat up. Far off in the gathering gloom glowed a solitary pinpoint of yellow-orange light. Another campfire. He rose to his feet.

The women looked in the direction he was looking and all three stood and clustered around him.

"What do you think?" Sister Angelina asked.

"Could be anyone," Fargo said. "Prospectors. Bandits. Soldiers."

"Apaches?"

"They're too smart to make a fire where it can be seen."

Dalila dismissed it with a gesture. "They're not anywhere near us so I don't see why you're so worried."

"They're not near us *now*."

Fargo sat back down. Presently the rabbit was done and

39

he passed out pieces of juicy meat to the ladies. They ate with their hands. Paloma held her piece as if it were fragile and took tiny, delicate bites. Dalila wolfed hers. Sister Angelina chewed slowly.

Fargo leaned on his saddle. They were safe for the moment and he could relax a bit. When the coffee was ready he poured a cup for himself and for Sister Angelina. The girls didn't want any. The wind had picked up, as it often did at night, and brought with it the keen of wolves and the cries of coyotes. Once a mountain lion shrieked. Other than that, the night was quiet.

A few times Fargo noticed Dalila looking at him as if she were studying him. When he looked at her she looked away.

Paloma was the first to say she was tired and lay down to sleep. Sister Angelina was next.

Fargo went on sipping and listening and after a while Dalila glanced at her sister and the nun as if to assure herself they were asleep, and turned toward him.

"You are very handsome, senor."

Fargo swirled the coffee in his tin cup.

"Didn't you hear me? I said you are handsome."

"You're sitting right there."

Overhead, a meteor streaked the sky.

Dalila quietly stood, came around the fire, and sank down beside him. "Now I am right here."

"What are you up to?"

"What do you think?" Dalila rejoined, and placed her hand on his thigh. "I would like for us to become better acquainted."

"Been with a lot of men, have you?"

Dalila lost her grin. "What does that have to do with anything? I find you attractive. That should be enough."

"Oh really?" Fargo put down the tin cup and covered her beasts with his hands and squeezed. She went rigid with surprise, and pulled back.

"Senor!"

Chuckling, Fargo picked up his cup again. "Quit playing at something you're not."

Dalila seemed confused. "Don't you want me?"

"Any man would," Fargo said. "How many have you made love to?"

"There you go again," Dalila huffed. "But for your information, I have lain with more than you have fingers and toes."

Fargo choked off a belly laugh so as not wake the others. "Liar. The most you've ever done is daydream and touch yourself."

"Senor!" Dalila blushed a deep red. "You are no gentleman."

"Never claimed to be." Fargo leaned toward her. "Ordinarily I'd be glad to hike those skirts of yours. But I gave my word to the nun to protect you, and that includes protecting you from me."

"That's silly, senor."

Fargo shrugged and sat back. "A man's word should mean something or he's not much of a man."

Dalila fell silent. Several minutes went by before she coughed lightly and said in a near-whisper, "I have a confession to make."

"This should be good."

"I am serious. You mock me, yet only you can save me from a fate worse than death."

"This should be really good."

Dalila slid closer so their shoulders brushed and her face practically touched his. "We must keep our voices down so Sister Angelina doesn't hear."

"I'm listening."

"I don't want to be a nun, senor. You already know that. I argued and argued with my mother but she wouldn't listen. I appealed to my father but he always does whatever mother wants."

"She wears the britches in your family."

"Britches? Oh, I see. Yes. My mother had always decided what the rest of us will do. She decided when I was little that I would be a nun one day. I hate the idea. I told Sister Angelina I hate it. But she said I must honor my mother and father and do as they ask. So here I am."

"You could have said no."

Dalila shook her head. "You don't understand, senor. As much as I want to, I can't. She is my mother. I must do as she bids me."

Fargo never could savvy why some folks let others ride roughshod over them. He never let anyone tell him what to do.

"I am in what you would call a predicament. But there is a way out, a way for me to keep from becoming a nun without disobeying my mother."

"Well, try that then," Fargo said.

"It's why I am talking to you," Dalila said. "You see, my way out is you."

"What the hell can I do?"

"How do I put this?" Dalila said, more to herself than to him. "One of the, ah, requirements for becoming a Sister of Apostolic Grace is that the candidate can't be tainted. Pure in mind and body is how Sister Angelina put it."

Fargo saw where this was leading. "The women have to be virgins." He wondered how they tested to prove it.

"*Sí*. My sister and I have never been with men. So if I was to lie with one before we reach the convent, I would not be acceptable. The nuns would turn me away. It wouldn't be the same as openly defying my mother, and it would leave me free to live the kind of life I desire to live."

"You can't be saying what I think you're saying."

Dalila put her hand back on his thigh. "I want you to fuck me."

7

New Mexico was an oven. The sun burned in a cloudless sky, baking the land and every living thing. Even in the mountains the temperature pushed one hundred. Which was why by the middle of the morning Fargo drew rein on a rocky ridge, took off his hat, and mopped his face and brow with his bandanna.

Sister Angelina was next to reach the crest. She and her mule were weary from the climb. She smiled her sweet smile and said, "Why have you stopped? I'm not in need of rest."

"The animals are." Fargo dismounted and arched his back to relieve a kink and moved to where he could see down their back trail for many miles. The dun went past him, Dalila handling the reins, her sister behind her. Dalila had avoided meeting his eye since last night. Probably because after she told him what she wanted, he'd told her to turn in.

She had been incredulous. "I've just thrown myself at you and you want me to go to sleep?"

"I'll think about the offer."

"Think?" Dalila had said as if she could not believe her ears. "Here you are supposed to be so fond of the ladies."

"Who told you that?"

"Mother Superior. The *coronel* warned her about you. He said you have never met a woman you did not want to bed. Is that true?"

"No," Fargo said. He had his standards. Of more interest to him was the fact that Sister Angelina had sought him out anyway.

Now, shielding his eyes with his hand, he searched for sign of dust or movement in the vastness below.

Sister Angelina climbed down and joined him. "Anything?"

"Not so much as a fly."

"We are making good time. At this rate we will reach the convent a day sooner."

"Good." The sooner Fargo was shed of them, the sooner he could treat himself to whiskey and a dove. He turned and she placed a hand on his arm.

"One moment. Is there something going on between Dalila and you that I should know about?"

"Not a damn thing."

"Are you being truthful with me? I've seen how she looks at you, and she is a most attractive young woman, yes?"

"Sort of," Fargo said.

"Her hair, her body, most men would drool over her," Sister Angelina went on as if she hadn't heard. "It would not surprise me if you were drawn to her."

"I just told you nothing is going on." Fargo resented her implying he was a liar. "I won't touch your precious nuns."

"They are not nuns yet," Sister Angelina said. "So you may touch them as much as you want." She smiled her sweet smile and moved toward the sisters.

"What the hell?" Fargo said. He scratched his chin in bewilderment. Had she just given her consent? That was what it sounded like, but it couldn't be. He went to go to the Ovaro but stopped. To the south tendrils of dust were rising. Not a lot. Enough to suggest two or three riders. Riders who could be on their trail.

"My throat is parched," Dalila announced, and stepped to the Ovaro to take the water skin down.

"I'll do that," Fargo said. She might spill some, and every drop wasted was less for the rest of them. He unhooked the bag from the saddle horn, opened it, and held it so she could tip it to her mouth as easily as a foal might suck a teat. Her throat bobbed several times, and he stepped back. "That's enough."

"I'm still thirsty."

"You'll wait until we make camp for the night." Fargo turned to her sister. "How about you?"

"I am fine, senor," Paloma said.

"You don't drink enough, you could pass out from the heat."

"I am fine, I said."

Fargo turned to the nun. "Your turn."

"I am fine as well," Sister Angelina said. "At my age I do not need much."

"Now who is fibbing?" Fargo said. The heat was always worse for the old and the young. He plugged the waterskin and hung it over the saddle horn. "It's here if you change your minds." Shucking the Henry from the saddle scabbard, he went back and hunkered. The dust tendrils were closer. He still thought it was only two or three. They were coming on fast.

"What are you looking at?" Sister Angelina asked.

Fargo pointed. "We'll likely have company before too long."

Sister Angelina squinted against the glare. "Goodness, you have good eyes. I can barely make that out. What do we do?"

"Wait to see who they are."

"Is that wise? Shouldn't we push on as fast as we can?"

"And tire our horses so we're easy to catch?" Fargo shook his head. "This is as good a spot as any." The climb to the crest was mostly open save for a few boulders. He could hold off a large force so long as his ammunition lasted. "Tell the girls to make themselves comfortable. Shouldn't be more than ten minutes and we'll know what's what."

"Very well," Sister Angelina said, but she did not sound happy about it.

Fargo cradled the Henry close to his chest so the sun wouldn't reflect off the brass receiver and give him away. Sweat trickled down his back and legs. Sweat trickled down his forehead. A drop got into his left eye and stung like the dickens. He blinked to clear it.

He had been right. There were three of them, riding hard. He worked the lever to feed a cartridge into the chamber.

Sister Angelina and the girls hurried over. She stared at the rifle and said, "You're not going to shoot them down, are you?"

"Depends on who they are."

"We don't *know* who they are," Sister Angelina stressed.

"You can't just up and shoot them. We must talk to them. Find out what they want."

"It's too dangerous to let them get close."

"You begin to worry me, Senor Fargo. Protecting us is one thing. Shooting people without cause is another."

The riders were near enough that Fargo could see two of the three wore sombreros. The third wore a flat-crowned brown hat. The brown hat was in the lead, and apparently the tracker; he repeatedly bent to read the sign.

"Stay back out of sight," he cautioned the ladies, and stepped to where the riders could see him. Almost immediately one of the sombreros pointed and the three drew rein. Fargo held the Henry in plain sight, his finger on the trigger.

The man who had pointed pushed his sombrero back on his head. He had curly black hair and a thick mustache. *"Buenas tardes,* senor!" he hollered up.

Fargo didn't say anything.

"Habla usted español?" the man shouted.

Fargo did but he didn't reply.

"English then, eh? Very well. We will speak that. I am called Yago. How are you called?"

Fargo cupped a hand to his mouth. "Turn around and fan the breeze."

Yago cocked his head. "That is not very friendly, senor. My amigos and I mean you no harm."

Leveling the Henry, Fargo said, "I won't tell you twice."

Yago said something to his companions. Both forced smiles to try and show they were friendly. Yago tapped his spurs and his claybank started toward the crest.

Fargo fired into the ground in front of it. The horse, startled, shied, but Yago prevented it from running off and patted its neck to calm it. The other two had their hands on their six-shooters.

The man with the brown hat, who had a bushy beard and bulbous cheeks, also had a voice like the growl of a bear. "That wasn't very friendly, mister."

"Move on," Fargo said, levering a cartridge into the chamber.

"You can't go around telling folks what to do," the man shouted back. "Who the hell do you think you are?"

Fargo wedged the rifle to his shoulder and took deliberate aim. "I'm the son of a bitch who will blow your brains out if you don't get the hell out of here."

Yago said something to the others out of the corner of his mouth. Then he smiled and held his hands out. "Very well, senor. I do not like how you treat us but we will go."

Fargo kept the rifle wedged. They reined around, or started to, then unexpectedly stopped and stared up at him as if in surprise. Suddenly he realized it wasn't him they were looking at, and he glanced to his left.

Sister Angelina had stepped to his side and was standing with her small hands clasped to the crucifix she wore around her neck.

"Damn it," Fargo said. "I told you to stay back."

"I wanted to be sure," she said.

"Sure of what?"

"So you are not alone, eh, gringo?" Yago called up. He rose in the stirrups to see her better and switched to Spanish. "I know you, old woman. I have seen you before."

"Yes," Sister Angelina responded. "You have."

"You are from the convent."

"I am the Mother Superior."

"Yes. I remember that, too. Everyone says you are kind and decent." Yago paused. "What are you doing with the gringo?"

"Don't tell him," Fargo warned.

"I am on my way back with supplies," Sister Angelina shouted. "This man is helping me."

"Are nuns supposed to lie?" Fargo asked her.

"Hush."

"I see," Yago called up. "Very well, Mother Superior. We will let you go in peace." He spoke to the others and they headed back down the trail.

Fargo lowered the Henry. "Showing yourself was dumb."

"They are leaving, aren't they?" Sister Angelina countered. "Besides, I thought I recognized the voice of the one who called himself Yago. He is a well-known bandit. He has done many despicable things."

"I would never have guessed," Fargo said dryly.

"He rides with Fermin Terreros."

"The gent who rapes nuns."

Sister Angelina nodded. "Those other two men must be bandits too." She gnawed her lower lip, watching them ride away. "It is just bad luck they have found us."

"Bad luck, hell," Fargo said. "They probably keep a watch on the trails out of Santa Fe."

"For people to rob and kill, you mean?"

"What else?" Fargo went to the Ovaro, shoved the Henry into the scabbard, and climbed on. The women followed his example.

At the bottom of the ridge the trail forked.

"We bear to the right," Sister Angelina let him know.

The trail climbed and dipped and climbed again. Often they rode over solid rock, the shod hooves of the horses pinging like hammers.

There was no sign of pursuit but Fargo wasn't fooled. The bandits wouldn't make the same mistake twice.

By sunset the women were worn out and the dun and the mule were flagging. Fargo made camp on an outcropping that afforded a sweeping vista. For fuel there were clusters of brush. He heated coffee and passed out pieces of jerky from his saddlebags.

Dalila scrunched up her nose and regarded her piece as if it were a bug. "Is this all we are having?"

"Unless you want to go hungry," Fargo said, chewing hungrily.

Sister Angelina pointed. "Look. Is that them?"

A mile off, maybe less, another fire glowed.

"That's them," Fargo said.

"What will they do? Sneak up on us while we sleep? Or perhaps spring on us from ambush?"

"To do that they have to get ahead of us," Fargo said. "Is there another trail that would let them do that?"

"Not that I know of," Sister Angelina said. "And I have lived in these mountains many years."

"Then it will be tonight or tomorrow night," Fargo suspected.

"Do you think they know about my sister and me?" Paloma asked.

"Wouldn't surprise me," Fargo said. "You three get some

48

sleep. I'll keep watch and wake you an hour or so before dawn. If we get an early start maybe we can keep ahead of them until we reach the convent." Not that he believed that for a moment.

Sister Angelina said, "It's not fair that you bear all the burden. We will take turns sitting guard."

"Better that I do it," Fargo said. He didn't trust them not to doze off. "Go ahead and rest."

Sister Angelina was disposed to argue but she reluctantly gave in. Presently all three were under their blankets and exhaustion took its toll.

Fargo held his warm tin cup in his hand and stared at the other fire. It wasn't all that far. On foot he could get there and back in an hour or so. He drank more coffee, and pondered. The bandits would bide their time and pick the best spot—if he let them. It would be stupid to let them.

Fargo set down the cup and drew his Colt. Normally, he loaded five cartridges in the cylinder. A lot of men did the same. Dropped pistols were known to go off if there was a round under the hammer. He only ever added a sixth when he knew he might need the extra shot. He added a sixth now.

Draining his cup, Fargo opened his saddlebags and put it in. He took off his spurs and put them in, too. Rising, he stared at the women. Sister Angelina, with her many wrinkles; Dalila, as sensual and desirable as when she was awake; Paloma, angelic in the rosy glow of the firelight.

Fargo laid the Henry next to Sister Angelina. In the dark the Colt would do him just as well. He went past the horses to the trail. A stiff gust of wind brought a brief chill. Then he started down.

There were six bandits now, not three.

Yago and the man in the brown hat and the other one had been joined by three curly wolves cut from the same cut-throat cloth. Hunkered around the fire, they were passing a bottle of tequila back and forth, and talking and joking. They were in good spirits. With good reason, as Fargo learned when he crawled to within a stone's throw of the crackling flames. One of the newcomers was talking.

"Were it up to me, we would jump them tomorrow. There's only that one gringo you saw."

Yago was taking a swig of tequila. He lowered the bottle and wiped his mouth with his sleeve and said, "What will you tell Fermin, Bartolo? That you forgot we were to wait until he and the rest catch up to us?"

The man in the brown hat barked a cold laugh. "And after Fermin slits your throat, we'll roll dice for your horse and your guns."

"And leave you to rot," said another.

"I never said we should go against Fermin," Bartolo said. "Do not put words in my mouth."

"Be more careful with your tongue, then," Yago said harshly. "Or have you forgotten Pedro? All he did was say that Fermin should let us go to town more, remember? Fermin shot him."

"Blew his head clean off," said the man in the brown hat. "Anyone bucks Terreros, or he even *thinks* anyone is bucking him, they're maggot bait."

"Slate is right," Yago said. "Fermin is the most vicious hombre I've ever met." He grinned. "That is why I ride with him."

Bartolo decided to change the subject. "Do you think the gringo knows that you saw the two *chicas*?"

Yago turned and reached into a saddlebag and brought out a brass spyglass. He raised it to his right eye and extended the telescope to its full length, and chuckled. "I very much doubt it."

One of the other bandits gleefully rubbed his hands together. "I can't wait to have my turn with them."

"Maybe you would rather have the nun?" another bandit said, and all of them laughed except Yago.

"No one touches her."

They looked at him.

"You heard me. I know of her. She is the Mother Superior at the convent. She heals the sick and helps the poor. No one touches her or they answer to me." Yago placed his hand on an ivory-handled Remington on his hip.

"Hell, Yago," Slate said in jest. "I never took you for religious."

"I stopped going to church when I was ten and my parents died. But I will not kill a priest or a nun and I will not stand by and let them be harmed."

"Fermin might have a different notion," Slate remarked.

"Yes," Yago said. "He might."

They were silent a while. Then Yago took another swig of tequila and passed the bottle to Bartolo. "Fermin should catch up to us by tomorrow afternoon. We will kill the gringo and take the *chicas* tomorrow night."

Fargo had heard enough. He worked his way wide around the circle of firelight and near to their mounts. Instead of a rope picket, each animal had been hobbled to keep it from straying.

Sliding his hand into his boot, he drew the Arkansas toothpick from its ankle sheath. The twin razor edges would make short work of the hobbles. He stalked forward but took only a few steps and stopped.

A sorrel had raised its head and pricked its ears in his direction.

Fargo had to be careful. All it would take was one whinny to give him away. He stayed frozen until the sorrel lowered its head. Quickly, he took another couple of steps.

The same sorrel raised its head again.

Fargo stayed still until it lost interest and was dozing. Or so he thought. He moved slowly forward but no sooner did he take a step than the sorrel jerked its head high and nickered in alarm. Instantly, he flattened.

The bandits all looked toward the horses. Slate stood and said, "I think that was mine. Likely smells a cougar. I'll go have a look."

Fargo hugged the ground. He was about ten feet from the animals so he should be safe from being spotted.

Slate had his hand on his revolver. He patted the sorrel and said, "What has you bothered, boy?" He peered into the dark.

"What is it?" Yago asked.

"Hell if I know." Slate returned to the fire. "I didn't see anything."

Fargo let several minutes go by. The sorrel didn't whinny when he rose but it looked at him. So did a chestnut and a

51

grulla. The grulla appeared to be the calmest so he went to it first and bent to the hobble, and sliced. He was so intent on what he was doing that if not for the jingle of a spur, he wouldn't have looked up.

Slate had come back and was rooted in surprise. "You!" he blurted, and clawed for his six-gun.

Fargo dived around the grulla. He rolled and was up and running even as Slate bawled to his friends.

"Over here! It's the guy in buckskins!"

A shot boomed and lead nearly took Fargo's hat off. He raced flat out even though he couldn't see more than a few feet. The bandits were shouting and had given chase. A boulder loomed and he darted behind it and switched the toothpick to his left hand and drew the Colt. Dark figures were converging. Flame stabbed the night and a slug whined off the boulder. He fired at the shooter and had to duck down as four or five revolvers cut loose at once. There were too many. He could make a fight of it but their numbers would tell. Whirling, he sped off in long bounds, a two-legged antelope with a pack of wolves nipping at his heels. Pistols cracked. The bandits did more yelling. He was going pell-mell when the ground seemed to give way under him. He tried to catch himself but his own momentum pitched him to the bottom of a dry wash. He hit hard on his shoulder with the breath knocked out of him.

"Where is he?" someone shouted in Spanish.

Boots thudded and spurs jangled.

"Don't let him get away!" Yago bellowed.

A shape appeared above. Fargo tried to raise the Colt but his arm was numb from the fall.

"I don't see him!" the shape shouted.

"He can't have gotten far!"

The shape turned and melted into the murk.

Fargo used his good arm and wriggled up with his back to the other side. The numbness was fading but not fast enough. From the sound of things, the bandits were crashing around like enraged bulls.

"Bartolo, bring a torch!" Yago yelled.

Fargo had to get out of there. He got his legs under him and stood and followed the wash until he was almost out of earshot. He slid the toothpick into his ankle sheath but kept the Colt in his hand. Eventually he reached the top of the ridge.

All three women were up, Dalila and Paloma with blankets over their shoulders. Sister Angelina wagged a finger and demanded, "Where have you been? We heard shots."

"I tried to run their horses off." Fargo sat and poked at the embers. He added brush and blew on the tiny flames and then placed the coffeepot on to reheat. His arm had stopped tingling but his shoulder was sore.

"We were worried, senor," Dalila said.

"I was worried too."

Sister Angelina did more finger wagging. "We are serious. You could have been killed. Where would that leave us?" When Fargo didn't answer, she said, "I'll tell you. It would leave us at their mercy. Give me your word you won't try anything like that again."

"No."

"I beg your pardon."

"I won't give my word if I know I can't keep it." Fargo rubbed his shoulder and gazed down the mountain. Half a dozen fireflies flitted about—the bandits with their torches, still searching.

"When I asked you to protect us, I didn't mean for you to lose your life in the attempt," Sister Angelina said.

"Then you were fooling yourself," Fargo said.

The nun's wrinkles doubled. "That is a terrible thing to say."

Fargo wished the coffee would get hot. "You can't have it both ways. You can't expect me to spill blood to keep you alive and not expect whoever is out to hurt you to not to try and spill my blood."

"Somehow I thought you could keep us safe without any blood being spilled on either side."

Damned if she wasn't serious, Fargo realized. He chuckled and shook his head. "That's what comes from living up in the clouds, I reckon."

"I am a practical person, I'll have you know," Sister Angelina said defensively.

"Practical, hell." Fargo took a breath, and decided to be

nice to her. "Listen, Sister. You live by what the Bible says, and your church. Love one another. Do good by your neighbor. Those sorts of things. But that's not how the real world is. Out here"—Fargo gestured to encompass the Sangre de Cristos and the rest of creation—"people don't always love one another or give a damn about doing right. Out here, they kill one another. Out here, they steal their neighbors' money and their land. Out here isn't like it is behind the walls of your convent."

"I know that. I'm not a fool, after all."

"Never said you were."

The nun turned and went to her blankets and laid down with her back to them and pulled the top blanket to her shoulder.

"That was a terrible thing to say to a woman like her," Paloma said to him.

"She's dragging you two off to be nuns and you're standing up for her?"

"I want to be a nun, I'll have you know," Paloma declared. "Mother Superior doesn't have to drag me."

Down below, the fireflies were gathering around the bandit's campfire. They had given up.

Fargo was tempted to sneak back down later and pick off as many of them as he could.

"You are not nice, I think," Paloma wouldn't let it drop, and wheeled on her heel. "I am going back to sleep. Are you coming, Dalila?"

"In a minute."

Fargo stretched. He was tired and sore and had a long night ahead. "Are you just going to stand there and stare?"

"I can't help it. You are so handsome," Dalila whispered, and eased down an arm's length away. "It makes it easier for me. If you were ugly, I might not want you to save me from the convent."

"Lucky me," Fargo said.

"You don't find me as attractive as I find you?" Dalila thrust her shoulders back so her bosom swelled and ran a hand enticingly down her leg.

"Now's not the time."

"My sister and Mother Superior will soon be asleep. We could go off a little ways."

"Just like that?" Fargo said, and snapped his fingers.

"I'm not afraid. I look forward to it." Dalila grinned and rimmed her red lips with the tip of her tongue. "Don't pretend you don't want me. You're a man, and men can't keep it in their pants."

"Says the girl playing at being a woman."

Dalila surprised him by cupping her breasts. "Tell me I am wrong. Tell me you don't want me as much as I want you."

Fargo couldn't for the lump in his throat. He felt himself stir below his belt.

"I didn't think so," Dalila said, and laughed.

From out of the north came a wavering howl. The dun nickered. Paloma rolled over so her back was to them.

Dalila lifted her face to the stars and inhaled. "It is a fine night for it, yes? A night I will always remember."

"Until the next man," Fargo said.

"Have you no romance in your soul? No passion in your heart? A woman never forgets her first time."

"How would you know?"

"It is what I have been told and I believe it. Maybe it's not true for a man but it is true for a woman."

Fargo thought of something. "You told me that you're doing this so you won't have to be a nun."

"So?"

"How will the sisters at the convent know you're not a virgin? Do they have you lie down and hike your dress and take a peek?"

"That is disgusting."

"Then how?"

"I will tell them. I will say that you had your way with me. That I tried to resist you but you were too big and strong and there was nothing I could do."

"You're going to tell them I raped you?"

"I won't call it rape," Dalila said. "But I must give the impression it was your idea and not mine. Otherwise my mother would never forgive me."

"The more you tell me, the less I like it," Fargo said. Still, she *was* a looker, and willing, and he supposed he could handle a passel of riled nuns.

As if she could read his thoughts, Dalila said, "Now who is fooling himself? You try to hide it but I see the hunger in your eyes."

The fireflies down the mountain had winked out. Only the twin glows of the two campfires broke the vast sea of darkness.

Dalila glanced at the sleeping forms of her sister and the nun, and leaned toward him. "I want to hear you say it. What will it be, yes or no?"

Fargo drank in the sight of her; from the lustrous sheen of her hair to the bulge of her bosom to the alluring curves of her hips and the long sweep of her thighs, she was exquisite. "Your sister's not the only one who asks stupid questions."

8

Stillness gripped the night.

Sister Angelina was snoring. Paloma hadn't moved in over half an hour. Their fire was low. The brisk wind had died and the wolves and coyotes had fallen silent.

Skye Fargo stood and walked from the fire into the veil of ink. Without being asked, Dalila followed. She wore a bold, almost brazen expression, as if she did this sort of thing all the time. A nervous tic to her mouth and the way her fingers kept twining suggested otherwise.

Fargo wasn't worried the bandits would pay them a visit. From what he'd overheard, Yago and his friends were to sit tight until Fermin Terreros showed up.

When he was sure they had gone far enough, he turned. His eyes had adjusted and he saw her flash a nervous smile. He also admired the contours of her luscious body. He put his hands on his hips and waited for her to make the first move.

Dalila coughed. "Well," she said.

"I'm plumb out of flowers," Fargo said.

"Those would be nice, wouldn't they? But I guess a girl can't have everything." Dalila fiddled with a button. "I'm sorry. But now that we're about to do it, I want to run off and hide."

"No one is forcing you."

"That doesn't make it easier." Dalila ran her hands along her arms as if to warm them. "You must think I'm being silly."

"Some things can't be rushed."

"Thank you." Dalila looked at the ground and at the stars and back at their fire and at the bandit fire, but not him. "God," she said. "I had it all worked out in my head, how it would go. I would say I was ready and you would take me in your arms and smother me with hot kisses and then lay me

57

down and you would know just what to do, and I would, too."

"One of us does," Fargo said. "The other only thinks she does."

"I haven't told you this before but you are wise for a gringo."

"I'm also getting hard."

"How do you . . ." Dalila glanced at the junction of his legs and lightly exclaimed, "Oh. I see what you mean."

Fargo was willing to be patient with her although her jabber was grating on his ears. "Either we do or we don't."

"Please," she said.

"Life is never simple."

"I am not as cynical as you. My family is poor but until this happened I have had a good life." Dalila gestured at him. "I just can't believe I am throwing myself at you."

"If this is throwing," Fargo said, "I'd hate to see when you crawl."

"Must you mock me? Can't you tell I'm scared?" Dalila's next comment was barely audible. "More scared than I have ever been."

"Slow and easy does it," Fargo said, and reaching out, he pulled her to him. She came willingly into his arms. He hugged her and felt her tremble like a frightened fawn. Gently, he ran his hand over her hair and down her back. She went stiff from head to toe.

"I don't know if I can do this, senor."

"You want to stop, you only have to say." Fargo lightly kissed her hair and her forehead and her cheek. Her eyes were as wide as walnuts. He placed a hand on her leg above the knee and she gasped so he took it off again.

"Oh God," she said.

Fargo let go of her. "If you're this afraid, maybe we should stop. Save yourself for your husband."

"If we stop I will never have one," Dalila said. "I will be cursed to wear a habit the rest of my life."

"We can always pretend. Tell the nuns we made love and when they ask me I'll say it's true."

"You would lie for me?"

"I'll stretch the truth when there's good cause," Fargo

said. "You shouldn't have to spend the rest of your life miserable."

"My own sentiments, senor," Dalila said. "I will do what I must." Suddenly she pressed against him so they were flush from shoulders to hips and turned her face up to his. "Please," she said. Then again, almost pleading, *"Please."*

Fargo kissed her. He thought she might hold back but she returned the kiss fiercely, grinding her lips so hard, it hurt. He was the one who broke it and said, "No need to be so rough."

"Show me how. Show me everything."

Cupping her chin, Fargo kissed her several times, the touch of his lips as light as a feather. He kissed her cheek and her neck and nipped an earlobe. She shivered, then did the same to him. Fargo slid his hands to her lower back and she moved her hips invitingly. His right hand dropped to her backside, and she tensed again.

"A little too fast."

Fargo remedied that. He slowly kissed her mouth and slowly licked her throat and slowly slid his hand down and covered her bottom. She tensed again, but not as much. He kneaded her and locked lips. Her mouth parted, his tongue found hers, and they stayed locked in their embrace for a good long while.

Dalila pressed her brow to his chest and whispered something.

"I didn't hear what you said."

"That was nice."

"Want more?" Fargo teased.

Dalila's need got the better of her. Her next kiss was molten. Her body grew hotter.

She didn't touch him much, though, except to grip him by the shoulders. She was like a baby taking its first steps; unsure of herself, awkward, yet trying.

Fargo thought he heard a slight sound behind him. Spinning, he drew his Colt. It could have been a stealthy footstep.

"What is the matter?" Dalila whispered.

Fargo put a finger to her lips. She nodded and pressed against his side, against his right arm. Shifting, he pulled her around to his left. He didn't move after that, and thankfully she had the presence of mind to imitate him. The seconds crawled by, and at last he said, "I guess it was nothing."

"Don't do that to me," Dalila said. "I could hardly breathe. I was afraid it was bandits or Apaches."

Fargo slid the Colt into his holster and enfolded her in his arms. "Now where were we, pretty lady?"

Dalila wriggled and asked, "Are you sure it's safe?"

"If it wasn't I wouldn't do this." Fargo kissed her and cupped her bottom. She mewed as he lifted her bodily and ground himself against her. They fondled and caressed and explored, Dalila growing bolder with the passing minutes. When he squeezed a breast through her dress, she cooed. When he glided a hand down her thighs, she moaned. And when he slid the same hand between her legs and stroked, her fingernails dug into his arms.

Fargo's veins pulsed to the hammering beat of lust. He pried at her dress, baring her full twin globes. Shyly, she sought to cover herself but he gently brushed her hand away and swooped his mouth to a nipple. She rose onto the tips of her toes and pulled his head hard into her.

"Yessssss," she whispered.

Flicking and kneading, Fargo added to her arousal. She groaned and parted her legs wider to grant him access. He hiked her dress and the thin chemise she wore underneath and plunged his fingers up and under the warm folds. At the first brush she arched her back and her ruby lips parted. He thought she was going to cry out but she sank her teeth into his shoulder and moaned. He parted her nether lips. Suddenly she fastened her mouth to his as if to suck him into her.

Around them the night was a black mantle. Fargo knew he should stay alert for sounds and movement but he was losing himself in his need. His pole throbbed for release, and when she rubbed against him, he almost exploded.

Dalila said a few words in Spanish under her breath that Fargo didn't catch. He licked her neck, pulled her hair, sculpted her backside. Gradually their passion climbed until the tremulous moment on the cusp of entry. He lifted her and was poised to thrust but instead he penetrated her slowly. There was brief resistance, and moist velvet.

Fargo made their coupling last. He held off for as long as

he could, as long as he ever had. She became a thrashing cyclone of desire, her inhibitions shattered in the urgency of her craving. She bit him; she clawed him. They soared to a peak higher than the mountains, and then came the torrent. Dalila uttered a soft strangled sob, and gushed. It was the trigger for his release. He pounded and rammed and she locked her legs and rode him.

Exhausted, spent, they collapsed on the ground. She cuddled against him and he caressed her hair and closed his eyes. Sleep tugged at him, welcome rest after the long day, but he fought it off. Not yet, he told himself. Be smart.

"We have to get back."

"*Sí,*" Dalila said, but she made no move to rise or pull herself together.

"I mean it."

"*Sí.*"

Fargo gently shook her. "We can't stay out here by ourselves. Your sister and Angelina need guarding."

"*Mi hermana pequena,*" Dalila said dreamily, and giggled. "She really wants to be a nun. To waste her life in a prison."

"A convent doesn't have bars on the windows," Fargo said.

"It would be a prison to me." Dalila opened her eyes. "But now I can live a normal life. The life I want, and not as my mother wants." She gave him a hard, near-savage kiss. "I thank you from the bottom of my heart."

Fargo grinned. "Anytime."

"How about tomorrow night? And the night after that? And if I can persuade Mother Superior to let you take me home, every night until we get there."

"Damn, girl."

Dalila gave a toss of her head. "No, senor. I am a *niña* no longer. You have made me a woman."

"You helped," Fargo said.

She laughed and kissed his neck. "Amazing, is it not? Here we are, deep in the mountains with banditos after us, and this is the happiest moment of my life."

"Don't get too happy," Fargo cautioned. "Those bandits catch us, they'll turn us into worm food."

"Do not worry. I am not stupid. Mother Superior has told

me all about Yago and the man he rides with, that awful Fermin Terreros."

"What can you tell me about him? How long has he been robbing and killing?"

"For as long as I can remember," Dalila said. "Terreros is evil. They say he takes the lives of others like other men breathe. They say he likes it. He likes to hurt and to torture." She shuddered. "They also say that he and his men rape a lot of women. They rape them and then they cut them open and leave them to die."

She sounded so upset, Fargo looked her in the eyes and said, "I won't let that happen to you."

"Or Paloma, I hope. But you are one man and Terreros has twenty riding with him. All of them as vile as he is."

Fargo regretted not running off those horses. He had to come up with something else, and quickly. "Get dressed," he said, and rose. He hitched at his pants and settled his gun belt around his hips and patted the Colt.

Dalila moved slower. "I wish I could lie here with you the rest of the night. Just the two of us and the stars."

"Hurry up," Fargo said.

"What is your hurry?" Dalila smiled dreamily. "We have all the time in the world, my wonderful lover."

Fargo gazed down the mountain at the bandit's fire. "Not if they have anything to say about it."

Dalila began tying her chemise. "I was thinking about after we have taken my sister to the convent. Will you come live with us or will I come live with you?"

"What?"

She clasped his hand and pressed it to her bosom. "Now that I am yours and you are mine, we will be together forever."

"What in God's name are you talking about?"

"Us," Dalila said. "We can live with my mother and father until we find a place of our own. She will be mad at first but once she sees how much we care for each other and how good you are to me, she will accept you as her son-in-law."

"Oh, hell," Fargo said.

"What is wrong? You care for me, yes? Or you would not have made love to me with such fire."

"Sure I would," Fargo said.

Dalila delightedly squeezed him. "You are everything I hoped you would be, my handsome gringo."

"Oh, hell, hell."

"Why do you keep saying that? Surely you know that when a man and woman do as we have done, the man must do the honorable thing."

Fargo had been to Santa Fe before, and to southern California where Spanish culture still held sway. Those of Spanish stock were romantic by nature, and placed a high value on marriage. So much so, fathers were wrathfully protective of their daughters. A suitor who presumed to go too far was often compelled to walk the daughter to the altar at the point of a shotgun or a machete. "You never said anything about this before."

Dalila shrugged as if it were of no consequence. "I took it for granted you understood. Anyone would."

"You told me it was to save you from the convent."

"Yes, there is that, too."

"*Too?*" Fargo said.

"Why do you act so shocked?"

"There was more to this than you let on."

"The important thing is that I have wanted you since I first set eyes on you, and now I am yours forever and ever."

"Wonderful," Fargo said.

Dalila laughed and kissed him on the lips. "Yes, isn't it marvelous?"

9

The tendrils of dust had become a cloud.

Fargo had pushed hard since daybreak, or as hard as the women were capable of. Sister Angelina's mule was getting on in years, and like her, it couldn't go as far or as fast as it once did. The dun was bearing two riders and tired easily. If he was alone, he could outdistance the bandits handily. But now he had to stop much too often to let the mule and the dun rest.

Judging by the sun, it was about two in the afternoon when he drew rein at the edge of thick timber. "Stretch your legs if you want," he said, and dismounted.

The cloud was half a mile away, maybe less.

Sister Angelina had a hand to the small of her back, and winced. "I don't handle long rides as well as I used to."

"If you had any sense you'd have stayed in the convent and sent a younger nun to Santa Fe," Fargo told her.

"Why, senor, does that mean you care?" Sister Angelina chuckled but it died in her throat when she looked at the cloud. "They will catch us long before we reach the convent, won't they?"

"Yes," Fargo said.

"How soon, do you think?"

"Later today, probably."

"What can we do?" Sister Angelina worriedly asked. "I would never forgive myself if anything happened to my charges."

"You should have thought of that before you agreed to bring them into the godforsaken middle of nowhere."

"My, aren't you in a mood? But I suppose that is to be expected. Our lives are in your hands, after all."

"Thanks for reminding me."

"Now, now. I have every confidence in you and even more confidence that a higher power will see us through."

Fargo looked at her.

"You're not much for putting your faith in the Lord, are you?" Sister Angelina asked, not unkindly.

Fargo patted his Colt. "I put my faith in this."

"The kind of life you lead," Sister Angelina said thoughtfully, "your wits and your reflexes keep you alive, don't they?"

"I'm still breathing." Fargo switched his attention to the cloud and rubbed his chin.

"Do you have a plan? Or is it presumptuous of me to ask?"

"Presumptuous," Fargo said, and smiled.

"I read a lot," Sister Angelina said. "I use big words."

"I read tracks and whiskey labels."

"You underrate yourself. The *coronel* told me you are highly resourceful, as well as certain other things."

Fargo remembered what Dalila had told him and was going to ask her what those other things were but just then Paloma came over.

"Dalila went off into the woods. I said she shouldn't but she went anyway."

"Bodily functions can't be denied," Sister Angelina said.

"Oh, it wasn't that," Paloma said. "She just wanted to go for a walk."

"What?" Fargo wheeled and strode off after her, saying over his shoulder. "Stay with the animals. I'll be right back." He hurried but didn't spot her. He went at least sixty feet and opened his mouth to bellow her name, and she stepped from behind a tree.

"We need to talk, my handsome lover."

"We need to skedaddle," Fargo said, and crooked a finger. "Come on."

"Talk first," Dalila insisted. "Last night I could tell you were upset with me and I want to clear the air."

"Not now, damn it."

"Yes, now." Dalila gripped his hand and held it to her chest. "I don't want you mad at me. I want us to always get along."

Fargo wheeled and headed back without her. He glanced

65

around, and swore. She hadn't moved. "I will by God throw you over my shoulder and carry you if you don't move your little ass."

"Please don't talk to me like that. You must be gentle and romantic with me, as a lover should."

Fargo had warned her. He took two long strides and bent and scooped her onto his left shoulder. She was so astounded that she was slow to react. She bleated, "Let me go!" and pushed at his back and kicked. He held on.

"Please!" she pleaded. "I can't have my sister see me like this."

Stopping short, Fargo dumped her on the ground. She landed on her posterior with her hands flung behind her.

"The next time I tell you to do something, you do it. Our lives are at stake."

"Oh my," Dalila said.

Fargo held out his hand. "I'll help you up." She gripped his wrist and he pulled and she rose smoothly and pressed into him. He figured she would be angry but she was smiling. "What are you so happy about?"

"At how forceful you are. I've always dreamed of meeting a man who would sweep me into his arms and carry me away."

"I threw you over my shoulder."

"It's the same thing," Dalila said gaily. She grinned and winked and kissed his cheek. "I can't wait until we are alone tonight."

"Idiot." Fargo propelled her toward the horses. The dust cloud, to his consternation, was a lot closer. Her shenanigans had cost them. He shoved her at the dun and growled at her to climb on.

Sister Angelina and Paloma were already mounted. The nun was praying and Paloma was chewing on her lower lip.

"We ride like hell," Fargo commanded.

They tried. But the timber was so thick, and Sister Angelina and the girls were such poor riders, they might as well be turtles. He chafed at the slow pace but there was nothing he could do except urge them on.

Luck favored them in that the woods ended in a quarter of a mile. Above them canted a mostly open slope. Mostly, because here and there boulders rose, some as big as a Conestoga, others no bigger than a wagon wheel.

Fargo had an idea. Midway to the top he drew rein next to a boulder half as high as the Ovaro, and when Sister Angelina and the sisters reached him, he held out the reins to the nun and yanked the Henry from the saddle scabbard.

"What are you doing?"

"We need to whittle the odds." Fargo alighted. "Take the girls to the top and wait for me."

"Very well," Sister Angelina said. "But you must give me your word that you will be careful."

"What else would I be?"

The mule and the Ovaro climbed past but Paloma, at Dalila's bidding, brought the dun to a stop.

"I don't want you to do this," Dalila said. "You could be killed."

Fargo smacked the dun on the rump and it broke into a rapid walk. Dalila made as if to climb down and he jabbed a finger at her and snapped, "Don't you dare." He watched to be sure they kept going and once they were over the rim he slipped behind the boulder and propped his elbows on top. It wouldn't be long, he reckoned, and it wasn't.

Two men in sombreros came out of the timber first. One was a tracker. Hanging low from the saddle, he was reading the sign.

Behind them others appeared. Yago was there, and Bartolo, and the man called Slate. Only a few of the banditos were white. Two had the features of Indians, or else were half-breeds. They emerged and drew rein at the command of a rider on a magnificent palomino.

Fermin Terreros, Fargo guessed.

The man barked another command and Yago reached into his saddlebags and brought out his spyglass.

Fermin Terreros was what others would call a runt. He couldn't be more than an inch or two over four feet. He had wide shoulders but a body so thin, he was a broomstick. A thatch of gray hair poked from under his black sombrero. His shirt was white, his vest black with silver conchos. His gun belt sported conchos, too. His pants were black with orange stripes, on his boots were unusually large spurs. He had a thin mustache and a thin sprinkle of hair along his chin. The mark of age was stamped in the many lines on his face. All things considered, the terror of the Sange de Cristos looked about as fierce as a muffin.

The tracker and the other rider were almost to the boulder. Suddenly both men straightened and gazed up past it.

Fargo glanced up, too, and was astounded to see Sister Angelina standing in plain sight, her hands calmly clasped in front of her, smiling her serene smile.

Fermin Terreros saw her, as well. "Get her!" he shouted in Spanish, and the tracker and the other man tapped their spurs.

Fargo reared up. He had the Henry to his shoulder, the hammer already back. The tracker clawed for his revolver. The other man was a split instant slower. Fargo sighted and squeezed. The Henry boomed and the tracker was punched backward and sprawled in the dust.

Instantly, Fargo sent a slug into the other bandit.

Fermin Terreros raised an arm and opened his mouth wide.

Centering the Henry's sights on the small man's chest, Fargo yelled, "Anyone moves and you die!"

Terreros lowered his arm and closed his mouth.

"I can't miss at this range," Fargo stressed.

Fermin Terreros did an unusual thing: he grinned. In English he said, "You kill me, gringo, and my men will shoot you to pieces."

"Maybe so. But you won't be around to see it."

Terreros went on grinning.

"Keep your hands where I can see them and ride toward me," Fargo yelled. "Nice and slow. Your men are to stay right where they are."

Yago said something and Fermin Terreros shook his head. Another man spoke, and Terreros said, "Keep your wits about you." He gigged the palomino and came leisurely toward the boulder. He showed no fear. As he went by the two dead men he looked down. Then he gazed up at Sister Angelina and touched a finger to the brim of his sombrero. Not until he stopped did he focus on Fargo. "What now, gringo?"

"Two fingers, and two fingers only, take your six-shooter out and let it fall."

Terreros glanced at his holster. His pistol was a Smith & Wesson with ivory grips.

"Drop it in the dirt? I would prefer to hand it to you."

Fargo couldn't let himself be distracted. He had to watch the rest of the bandits, as well. "Do what I told you."

Continuing to grin, Terreros extended two fingers. He slowly wrapped them around the ivory grips and pulled the Smith & Wesson. It was an exceptionally fine revolver, with nickel-plating and engraving. Bending, he held it out.

"Drop it."

"No."

Fargo had the Henry fixed dead center on Terreros's sternum. "Are you hankering to die?"

"Only a fool wishes for extinction."

"Then drop the damn pistol."

"I had it custom-made, at great expense, by the best gunsmith in Mexico. I will not soil it for you or anyone else."

Fargo lowered the Henry a few inches. He saw no anger or hostility on the bandit leader's face, only the aggravating amusement. "You're loco to risk your life for a revolver."

"On the contrary, gringo, I am wiser than most. It is why I have lasted so long. *Por favor*. Take my *pistola*. I will not fight you."

Fargo didn't trust him. He hesitated.

"Listen to me, gringo. You can't shoot me because if you do my men will kill you. It is only the threat of you shooting me that holds them where they are. I also know that you *will* shoot if I force you, so I will not force you."

"You're not what I expected," Fargo said.

"I have heard that many times." Terreros wagged the Smith & Wesson. "I will be grateful."

Reluctantly, Fargo edged around the boulder, reached up, and snatched the revolver. None of the bandits below moved. He jammed the Smith & Wesson under his belt and stepped back so the boulder partially protected him.

"And now?" Fermin Terreros said.

"You're coming with us."

Terreros looked up at Sister Angelina. "With the holy one?" A strange expression came over him. "You are a friend of hers?"

"She hired me to get her to her convent."

"Did she indeed? How interesting."

"I'm taking you along as insurance," Fargo said. "Your men won't try anything so long as I have you."

Terreros was still staring at the nun. "The holy one will love you for this," he said, and laughed a peculiar sort of laugh.

"Tell your men to go back into the trees and stay there until we're out of sight," Fargo instructed. "Tell them that if they come within a mile of us from here on out, I'll shoot you dead."

"You intend to take me all the way to the convent?"

"I do."

"And once we are there?"

"I'll let you go. You have my word."

Fermin Terreros took his eyes from Sister Angelina. "You have a sense of honor, gringo. I admire that. And you are being reasonable. I admire that, too."

"I'm tickled pink."

"No need for sarcasm, gringo. I will do as you ask."

"Good. No one has to die if you're smart," Fargo said.

His saddle creaking, Terreros bent toward him. "You are a fool, gringo. Before this is done there will be blood."

10

Fargo followed Terreros up, the Henry trained on his back. He kept one eye on the rest of the bandits. They stayed by the timber, as they had been told, but it was obvious by their frowns and scowls that they didn't like it, not one little bit.

Sister Angelina didn't move. She smiled at Terreros as he came over the top. "Bandit," she said.

Fermin Terreros drew rein and stared at her with that peculiar expression. "Holy one," he replied. "The years have not been kind to you. You look like a prune."

"You look like half a prune," the nun said. "But then, men always age better than women—is that not so?"

"I feel old inside," Fermin Terreros said.

"While I feel young," Sister Angelina rejoined.

Fargo told Dalila and Paloma to climb on the dun. He swung onto the Ovaro. "Lead the way," he told Sister Angelina. "I'll bring up the rear." So he could cover Terreros and see if the bandits did as they were supposed to.

Yago and the others didn't move.

Fully three-quarters of a mile separated them when the trail led over a rocky spine and blocked the bandits from Fargo's sight. He could relax a little. He and the women were well out of rifle range.

So long as Fargo had Terreros, he had an ace in the hole. But the other bandits were bound to try something, sooner or later. The question was, what? And when?

The only other sign of life they saw all afternoon was a hawk on its aerial hunt.

In due course the setting sun stretched the shadows to preposterous lengths.

They made camp near another belt of woodland. Sister

Angelina and the girls gathered wood while Fargo watched Terreros. The bandit leader had not uttered a word for hours. Fargo had noticed that he gazed at the nun a lot and chalked it up to curiosity.

Once the fire was going, Fargo put coffee on to brew. They had some rabbit left and he warmed it, the Henry on the ground at his side, his right hand seldom far from his Colt.

Dalila and Paloma stared at Fermin Terreros as if he were a rabid wolf about to pounce. When he moved his hand to scratch his chin, they both gave a slight start.

"You are jumpy, young ones," Terreros said.

"We have heard about you," Dalila informed him. "Since we were little, people have told tales of the terrible things you do."

"Ah," Terreros said. "Wagging tongues. But the tales they tell are not always the full truth."

"They say you are a killer," Paloma said.

"I am."

"They say you have murdered men, women and children," Dalila said.

"Men and women but never children. There are limits to my evil."

Sister Angelina had been listening intently. Now she said, "That is good to hear. Perhaps it means there is hope for your soul."

"Ever the woman of God."

"Ever a heart of darkness," Sister Angelina said.

The bandit leader shrugged. "We make our choices. We must live with them. I have made peace with mine."

"Have you really? You have made peace with snuffing lives and all the thievery and the rapine ways of those who follow you?"

"Some of them are more evil than me."

"You are their leader, Fermin. Their wickedness rests on your shoulders as much as on theirs." Sister Angelina sadly shook her head. "To think. With your intelligence you could have been anything you wanted. Yet you chose a life of depravity."

"Now I am depraved?" Terreros said, and laughed. "Coming from the saint, it must be true."

"Don't start," Sister Angelina said.

"It has never ended," Terreros said.

Fargo had gleaned enough to interrupt. "What the hell is going on? The two of you know each other, don't you?"

Neither answered. They stared at one another until Sister Angelina cleared her throat.

"Yes, senor, we do. From a very long time ago."

"How did you know him?"

It was Terreros who answered. "We were lovers."

Dalila gasped.

Paloma showed the whites of her eyes.

About to reach for the coffeepot, Fargo blurted, "Son of a bitch." He stared at the nun. "You didn't think to tell me?"

"We weren't lovers in the sense you must be thinking," Sister Angelina said.

"I courted her," Terreros clarified. "When we were as young as these two." He gestured at the sisters. "I wooed her and asked for her hand in marriage."

"What happened that you didn't wed?" Dalila breathlessly asked.

Again neither answered right away. Again it was the nun who finally said, "He killed a man."

"Who insulted you," Terreros said. "He spoke of you as if you were a loose woman. I told him to apologize and he mocked me in scorn."

"So you shot him."

"It was a fair fight. He went for his gun, only I was too quick."

"You were always too quick," Sister Angelina said, "with your temper and with your *pistola*. I would have married you except for that."

Terreros looked at Fargo. "How do you like that? I defended her honor and she left me for defending it." He faced his former fiancée and his tone hardened. "It was as good an excuse as any."

"Excuse?" Sister Angelina repeated.

"*Sí*. You were always interested in the church. For a while

I thought you would choose me but when I defended you, you leaped at the chance to break off our engagement and wed yourself to the cross."

"Is that how you saw it?"

"It is how it was."

Fargo mulled what all this meant as far as getting the women to the convent in one piece.

"Tell me something," he said to Terreros. "Will you let Angelina be harmed?"

"You insult me, gringo."

"What about the girls?"

"They are nothing to me. They are less than nothing to my men. Playthings, to be used, and then to have their throats slit."

"Oh, Fermin," Sister Angelina said.

For the first time the bandit leader became angry. His features clouded and he speared a finger at her. "You have no right to sit in judgment. Not when you hide in your cloistered world."

"You make it sound sinful that I have devoted myself to the Lord."

"You are a coward, Angelina."

The sisters were thunderstruck.

Sister Angelina got up and walked off into the encroaching darkness, her head bowed. Dalila started to go after her but Fargo shook his head and said, "No." She sat back down.

"You're a mean man," Paloma addressed the bandit leader.

Fermin Terreros sighed and gazed into the flames. "You have your precious holy woman to thank for that. She jilted me because she thought as you do."

"Stop talking about her that way," Paloma said. "She is kind and wise. She loves everyone."

"Except me," Terreros said.

The Ovaro nickered. Fargo looked up, saw it peering past him. Instinct caused him to whirl and drop his hand to the Colt.

It was one of the bandits, one of the pair with Indian blood, swarthy and blocky and holding a bone-handled knife with a long blade.

Even as Fargo set eyes on him, the Indian sprang. Either

Dalila or Paloma screamed. Fargo cleared leather, thumbing the hammer back as he drew. Before he could fire the Indian slammed into him and he toppled onto his back with the Indian's knee on his chest and his hand clamped around the Indian's wrist. The tip of the knife was inches from his throat. Hissing, the Indian drove his arm down with all his strength and weight. Fargo held it at bay, and bucked. He wrenched his right arm free and jammed the Colt's muzzle against his attacker's chest and fired. But as he squeezed, the Indian jerked aside. The Indian clutched at the Colt and renewed his attempt to bury his blade.

Fargo expected Terreros to jump in at any moment. He braced for a blow to the head or to have his arms pinned. The Indian's face was contorted in fierce determination. The tip of the knife pricked Fargo's skin. Another few seconds and it would penetrate to his jugular.

Fargo shoved with all his might. He succeeded in flinging the Indian partway off but in a heartbeat the Indian slammed down onto his hips. Torment spiked his groin, and he came close to blacking out.

The Indian ripped his knife arm loose. Instantly, he stabbed at Fargo's throat. Fargo flicked his head aside and felt a slight sting. He thrust with the Colt, pressing the muzzle hard against the other's shirt. The Indian tried to throw himself back. At the blast he stiffened. At the second shot he keeled onto his side, briefly convulsed, and was still.

Scrambling to his knees, Fargo spun toward Fermin Terreros. The bandit leader was still by the fire. Where the sisters and the nun were staring at the dead man in horror, Terreros showed no more emotion than an adobe brick.

"That was Adoerte. He had Kiowa blood. You're lucky he only cut you a little. He was deadlier than most."

In raw fury Fargo surged to his feet. He took a step and kicked Terreros in the chest, bowling him over. Before Terreros could rise, Fargo jammed the Colt against his temple and clicked back the hammer. "You son of a bitch. I told them not to try anything or you would die."

Terreros grimaced and rubbed his chest. "I warned you earlier but you wouldn't listen."

Fargo stepped back. "Warned me about what?"

75

"Your bluff." Terreros slowly sat up.

Fargo aimed at the bandit's forehead. "I wasn't bluffing about killing you."

"Oh, you can pull the trigger, yes," Terreros said. "But the moment you do, my men will close in. All of them at once. Not like this." He nodded at the body of Adoerte.

"One at a time?"

"Or two or three."

"Son of a bitch."

"No matter what you do, you can't win," Terreros said. "You kill me, they'll kill you. You don't kill me, they'll kill you."

"Why didn't you help him?" Fargo wanted to know.

"It was his to do."

"You're a cold bastard."

Terreros smiled. "I don't have to lift a finger, and one after the other they will die for me, or kill you. My money is on them. You won't reach the convent, gringo. Neither you nor the *chicas*."

Fargo stared down the mountain into the inky abyss of the night. The bandits were down there, somewhere. He could practically feel their eyes on him. He suddenly ducked, mindful of being picked off at long range by a rifle.

Fermin Terreros chuckled. "Your death won't be that easy, gringo. They will get in close. They'll want to see your face when you die, and have you see theirs."

"Insanity," Sister Angelina said.

"Did you say something, my dear?"

"All this talk of killing," Sister Angelina said sadly. "All the killing itself. It is insane. You are not in your right mind, Fermin."

"On the contrary, my dear."

"Don't call me that. You lost the right when I donned my habit." Sister Angelina stepped to the dead man and felt for a pulse even though it was obvious he had given up the ghost. "Senor Fargo gave his word you would not be harmed if your men did not try to stop us from reaching the convent. Why can't your men accept that? Why can't you? Have you no shred of honor at all?"

"Don't speak to me of honor," Terreros said bitterly. "Did

you honor your pledge to take me as your husband?" He pointed at Adoerte. "As for this, we do it for real honor."

"How you twist words," Sister Angelina said.

"I am telling you true," Terreros said. "Were we to let this gringo use me, were we to let him have the better of us, we would lose the respect in which we are held."

"Respect?" Sister Angelina said, and laughed.

Terreros colored but contained his anger. "Yes, my former love. It is not the kind of respect you can understand but it is respect nonetheless. The people of Santa Fe, the farmers and ranchers, the Indians—yes, even the Apaches—they respect us because they fear us." He looked at Fargo. "And they fear us because no one has gotten the better of us."

"So you are saying you must kill Senor Fargo so that everyone else will go on fearing you?"

"To us, fear *is* respect."

"How could I have been so wrong about you all those years ago?" Sister Angelina sorrowfully asked. "I loved you. I truly did. I thought you were fine and noble. And then you went and shot that poor man and turned your back on all that is decent in this world."

"You turned your back on me first," Terreros said. "And without you, there was nothing I cared about."

"Excuses," Sister Angelina said.

Fargo bent and grabbed the dead man's wrists and dragged him from the circle of firelight and left him there. Let the bandits bury the body. He returned to the fire.

Terreros and Angelina were still arguing over their past.

Fargo shut them out. He had a more important concern: how to stay alive. One or two at a time, Terreros had said, and he never knew when or where. He swore, and realized the bandit leader and the nun had stopped squabbling and were staring at him.

"It dawns on you, doesn't it?" Fermin Terreros gloated.

"What does?" Sister Angelina asked.

"Come, my dear. Must you always miss the obvious?" Terreros was enjoying himself.

"It has occurred to your Senor Fargo that he is, as the gringos like to say, as good as dead."

11

The skin between Fargo's shoulder blades wouldn't stop prickling. He got a crick in his neck from glancing back. If the bandits were shadowing them—and there was no doubt they were—they were keeping well hid.

The sun beat relentlessly on the Sangre de Cristos. It was about eleven in the morning, and even at that altitude the air was sweltering.

The wildlife didn't mind the heat. A red-bellied marmot whistled and vanished down its burrow. Ten redheaded vultures wheeled high in the azure vault of sky.

Sister Angelina had said little all morning. Her charges did a lot of whispering and gave the bandit leader a lot of nervous looks.

Fermin Terreros, however, was in fine fettle. He smiled a lot, and whistled a lot, and whenever he noticed Fargo looking at him, he would chuckle and point a forefinger and lower his thumb, pretending to shoot. Once he ran his finger along his throat.

They were climbing to a pass that would take them into the next valley. On a distant cliff brown dots moved. Mountain sheep, Fargo suspected. Were they closer, and if he didn't have a pack of murderous coyotes nipping at his heels, he would try to drop one for supper.

A rocky slope rose to the pass. Sister Angelina had to goad her mule. Dalila and Paloma lashed the dun. Terreros stopped and pushed his sombrero back on his head and waited for Fargo to come up next to him.

"Keep going."

"A question first, if you will permit me," Terreros said with mock graciousness.

"Ask," Fargo said.

Terreros leaned on his saddle horn. "Are they worth it? Do you really want to die for two *chicas*? Why not make it easy on you and easy on me and my men, and go? Ride off and leave them to us. No one will ever know."

"I would."

"I repeat, are they worth your life?"

Fargo slid the Smith & Wesson from under his belt and held it out. "I suppose you'll be wanting this, too."

Terreros beamed. "I knew you would see reason. Give it to me and be on your way. I promise you are in no danger from me or my men." He reached across.

"Too bad I can't say the same."

"Eh?"

Fargo smashed him across the temple. Terreros dropped like a poled ox and his palomino, shying, nearly stomped on him. Fargo snatched the animal's reins and led it a dozen feet away. When he turned back, someone had already dismounted and was cradling the bandit leader's head in her lap.

"You shouldn't have done that," Sister Angelina said. "Whatever he said or did, violence isn't the answer."

"Tell that to him."

Scarlet trickled from a gash. Sister Angelina gently wiped it off and started to speak and it was a few moments before Fargo realized she was speaking to him and not Terreros. "I am sorry I involved you. I never imagined it would come to this. I honestly believed we could make it to the convent unnoticed."

"I'll do my best to get you there," Fargo promised.

Sister Angelina seemed not to hear him. "I thought that if Fermin did come across us, he would show more respect for me, and for what we once were."

Fargo had nothing to say to that.

"I am to blame, in part," Sister Angelina said. "When I turned my back on him, he turned his back on the rest of the human race." She stroked Terreros's brow. "Our mistakes always come back to haunt us, don't they?"

Before Fargo could reply, Paloma screamed, "Look out, senor!"

A hurtling form slammed into Fargo from the side. Unhorsed, he landed hard on his shoulder. Iron fingers gouged into his windpipe. It was another bandit, the second of the two with Indian blood. This one was stockier, and powerfully strong. Fargo pumped to his feet, or attempted to, and was smashed to the ground.

The Indian's mouth curled in a savage grin. "Your life is mine, white dog!"

Fargo struggled to breathe. His chest was in agony. He clawed for his Colt but the bandit's leg was in the way. His vision swam, and his strength ebbed, and he wondered if this was it.

Succor came from an unexpected quarter. Out of nowhere hurtled Dalila. She had a rock in her hand, and as the Indian looked up, she bashed him over the head. Blood spurted, and the Indian howled and leaped up, his hand sweeping to a knife on his hip. She went to strike him again and he grabbed her by the throat and drew his blade and raised it to stab her.

"No!" Sister Angelina cried.

By then Fargo had the Colt out. He fired into the bandit's chest. The Indian staggered and let go of Dalila. Fargo fired again and the Indian took a step back. He fired a third time, putting a hole above the Indian's nose, and the man folded.

"God," Dalila said.

Fargo slowly stood. His throat hurt like hell and he had a sharp pain in his back. "I'm obliged."

"I couldn't let him kill you. I didn't know what else to do."

"You did right fine."

Fermin Terreros groaned.

"Stand away from him," Fargo said to Sister Angelina. He began to reload.

"Senor?"

"You heard me."

"Why should I do that?"

When the third cartridge was inserted, Fargo shoved the Colt into his holster, stooped, and slid his hands under Terreros's arms.

"What are you doing?" Sister Angelina wanted to know. She tried to hold on to Terreros but Fargo tore him from her grasp, dragged him to the palomino, and proceeded to throw him over the saddle, belly down. He went to the Ovaro, claimed his rope, and unraveled it as he walked back.

"What are you doing?" Sister Angelina asked.

Fargo looped an end around Terreros's right wrist and tied a knot tight enough that it dug into Terreros's flesh. Then, passing the rope under the palomino, he tied it around Terreros's right ankle. Terreros was stirring when he wrapped the rope around the left ankle. As he was tying it to the left wrist Terreros opened his eyes.

"What is this? What are you up to, gringo?"

Fargo dallied the rope around the saddle horn, stepped to the Ovaro and climbed on.

"Why?" Sister Angelina asked, her voice quavering.

A tap of his spurs, and Fargo headed for the pass. He shortened his grip on the rope so that the palomino was only a few feet to one side.

"I asked you a question, gringo," Fermin Terreros said. "Answer me, damn you, or else."

"It's damned silly to threaten a man when your ass is in the air."

"This is undignified. Cut me down."

"What the hell would you know of dignity?"

"I've learned not to let others mock me," Terreros said. "If you are not careful, I will kill you myself."

"Speaking of killing, while you were out I killed your other Indian. I left the body for the buzzards."

Terreros's voice floated from under the palomino. "I am no longer amused by your antics. Cut me down, I say, or from this moment on we are enemies."

"We were enemies before we met."

For over an hour they rode in silence save for the pound of hooves. At the pass, Fargo called another halt to rest their mounts. They could see for miles, a spectacular vista of majestic peaks in serial ranks, sliced by deep valleys. A few of the peaks were white with a sprinkling of snow.

"It's so beautiful up here," Dalila said.

Fargo was checking the cinch on the Ovaro when Sister Angelina came up.

"How long do you intend to keep him like that?"

"Until hell freezes over."

"It's cruel. I implore you to show mercy. Let him ride as a man should."

"No."

"Why? Are you getting back at him for the men who tried to kill you? Is your motive so petty?"

Fargo resisted a twinge of resentment. "It's not petty to like breathing." He swept an arm at the slope they had climbed. "Yago has a spyglass. By now he's seen what I've done to your lover. They'll think twice about sending someone else."

The old nun's cheeks grew red. "He is nothing to me now. What was between us was many years ago."

"Then you shouldn't be upset."

"It's not him. It's what you have done. I would be upset if he did it to you."

Fargo let the stirrup down. "Time to go. You come last and keep watch behind us. You're in no danger. Terreros told them not to harm a hair on your head."

"You will not cut him free?"

"Maybe tonight if I feel like it."

"You are a hard man, Senor Fargo."

Fargo flicked his reins. Below the pass lay a valley green with grass, watered by a stream. Forest draped the lower slopes, promising game. He descended carefully, on the lookout for loose dirt.

Fermin Terreros coughed. "My stomach hurts, gringo."

"I don't give a damn."

"I am not to be trifled with. When I get the upper hand— and I will—you will suffer as few ever have."

"You take a lot for granted," Fargo said.

"How do you mean?"

"What makes you think I'll let you live that long?"

A wash appeared and Fargo reined into it. The bottom was littered with small stones and the going was easy. It also hid them from above. Halfway to the bottom he again reined up.

He drank from the waterskin and let each of the women have a turn. Sister Angelina was last, and after she wet her throat, she turned toward the palomino.

"No." Fargo took the waterskin.

"He has to be terribly thirsty."

"Tough." Fargo hung the waterskin on his saddle. He could feel her eyes boring into him.

"You would make a fine Apache, senor."

"I'll take that as a compliment," Fargo said. He climbed to the top of the wash and scanned the heights they had quitted. So far there was no sign of the bandits.

Dalila and Paloma joined him. Neither said anything until Paloma poked Dalila.

"We've been thinking, Skye."

"Oh?"

"We have a proposal for you."

Paloma nodded.

"You have Terreros in your power. You can make him do anything you want. Force him to give his word that if you cut him down, he and his men will leave and not bother us any more."

"We couldn't trust him," Fargo said.

"He claims he is a man of his word."

"Tell that to all those he's killed."

"Break his legs or his arms or both," Paloma suggested. "That will stop him from coming after us."

"But not his men."

"They will think twice if he is hurt."

"Like hell they will." Fargo paused. "Understand this, ladies. You're nothing to those bandits but tits and legs. They will fuck you and kill you no matter what we do with their boss."

"Oh, Skye," Dalila said.

Paloma turned her on her heel and stuck her nose in the air. "You are crude, senor. I will not listen to any more." Off she went.

"Forgive her," Dalila said. "She has never been as fond of the real world as she is of the world in her head."

"The bandits get hold of her, she'll wake up quick."

Dalila stood so their arms brushed. "They will come, won't they? No matter what we do."

"Yes."

"When?"

Up near the pass a flash of light gleamed. It was there and it was gone.

"Tonight," Fargo said. "When they think most of us are asleep. It won't be one or two. It will be all of them."

"What will you do?"

"Kill the sons of bitches."

Dalila swallowed hard. "I will help you. I have never fired a gun but if you show me what to do, I will fight by your side."

"I'll keep it in mind," Fargo said. "But I'm counting on someone else to lend a hand."

"Mother Superior? She would never agree. It is against everything she believes. Thou shalt not kill, the Bible says."

"Not her."

"Then who? My sister? I doubt she has it in her. She will not even kill a fly. She catches them and lets them out of doors."

"Not her, either."

Confused, Dalila said, "Who is there left?"

"The last person in the world the bandits would expect."

"Surely you don't mean . . ."

Fargo nodded.

"Fermin Terreros?" Dalila laughed. "One of us is loco, handsome one, and I'm afraid it isn't me."

12

Fargo needed the perfect spot. The bandits would be suspicious and wary. As he paralleled the blue ribbon on the valley floor, he studied the green forest on both adjoining slopes.

"I heard what you told the girl, gringo," Terreros said. "I will never help you against my men."

"Care to bet?"

"I can't wait for them to kill you so I can piss on your body."

"How's your head?" Fargo asked. "It must hurt like hell, hanging upside down like that for so long."

"*Bastardo*. I will have my men hold you down while I take a knife and slit your belly. I will rip out your intestines and stuff them down your throat. I have done that, you know, to others who made me mad."

"I'm going to make you madder."

The forest came closer to the stream on the right than on the left. At one point a needle of trees grew to within sixty feet of the bank. The finger was ten yards at its widest, narrowing near the water. There wasn't much undergrowth and the trees grew far enough apart that anyone could see in. Especially if they had a spyglass.

Fargo rode to a clear spot in the middle. Sliding down, he walked in a circle, debating.

Finally he turned to the palomino and quickly untied the knots that bound Terreros's wrists and ankles. "Climb down."

Terreros lay over the saddle like a limp cloth. His arms twitched, and he groaned. "You know I can't, you bastard. The blood has been cut off too long. I can hardly move."

"Let me help you."

Gripping a leg, Fargo tumbled Terreros to the ground. Terreros yelped and thrashed and cursed luridly.

"Senor Fargo!" Sister Angelina remonstrated. "Was that really necessary?"

"It felt good," Fargo said.

Terreros got his hands under him and attempted to stand but he couldn't rise more than a few inches. He sank down, his cheek in the dirt, and glared. "You pile insult on top of insult."

"Might as well add another, then." Fargo squatted and tied Terreros's ankles together. Then he roughly jerked Terreros's arms behind his back and bound both wrists. Hauling Terreros to his knees, he dragged him to a tree and secured the rope so that Terreros could hardly move. "There. You won't be going anywhere."

"Your mother was a whore."

"So was your father."

Fargo sat and tugged at his right boot. It took some doing to get it off. Setting it aside, he peeled off his sock.

"What are you up to now?" Sister Angelina asked.

"It needs washing," Fargo said. He rose, faced Terreros, and punched him in the stomach. Terreros doubled over, gurgling and wheezing, his mouth wide. So wide, it took a twinkling for Fargo to stuff the sock into Terreros's mouth. "That should keep you quiet."

Terreros's eyes bulged. He coughed and gagged and sought to spit the sock out but couldn't. His face became purple and spittle dribbled over his lip.

"Keep that up and you're liable to choke to death," Fargo said as he sat to pull his boot back on.

Terreros looked fit to vomit. He shook violently and uttered a strangled cry.

Sister Angelina moved to his side. "I can't let you do this. I can't let you abuse him this way." She reached down.

Fargo grabbed her wrist. "No."

"This is wrong," Sister Angelina said severely. "What possible purpose can it serve?" She sought to pull loose. "Please. Let go."

Fargo pulled her toward her mule. She resisted but he was too strong. He forced her to climb on and handed her the reins. "Stay there."

"It is despicable, I tell you."

"It's necessary," Fargo said.

The sisters were huddled on the dun. Lengthening shadows dappled them like funeral shrouds.

"What do you want of us?" Dalila asked.

"Follow me." Fargo forked leather, snatched the reins to the palomino, and made for the end of the valley.

The mule came to the Ovaro's side. "We must talk, senor."

"Now's not the time." Fargo had more urgent matters to attend to.

"I am sorry I ever asked for your help. You have proven to be as mean-spirited as Fermin, and more intractable."

"In-tract-a-what?"

"You refuse to listen to reason. Everything must be done your way. Our opinions are of no account."

"Not if they'll get us killed." Fargo spied a break in the slope wide enough for several horses.

"I must protest your treatment of Fermin. I grant you he is a bandito but he did not deserve to have your dirty sock shoved in his mouth."

"How many people do you reckon he and his men have bucked out in gore over the years?"

"I am sure I wouldn't know."

"Take a guess," Fargo prompted. "Twenty? Forty? Fifty or more?"

"I heard it said once that he is blamed for more than sixty."

"Sixty folks murdered. God knows how many women raped. And you're upset about a dirty sock?"

"Two wrongs do not make a right. Isn't that the expression?" Sister Angelina gazed back toward where they had left Terreros. "He is a bad man, I grant you, but . . ."

"No buts," Fargo cut her off. "He's vicious and mean and all those other things you accuse me of being. He's already told you that his men will rape Dalila and Paloma and you don't give a damn."

Sister Angelina appeared on the verge of tears. "That is simply not so."

"Prove it," Fargo challenged. "Show me you care more about the girls than you do about him."

"He is nothing to me."

"Bullshit. He's the man you once loved. The *only* man you ever gave your heart to, and deep down you still care. Deep down you blame yourself for what he's become and all he's done."

"You do not mince words, do you?" she said quietly.

They were almost to the break. Fargo reined over and the others filed in after him. He told them to climb down, and dismounted. He tied the reins to a low limb, slid the Henry from the scabbard, and opened a saddlebag to get extra ammunition.

"We are to stay here, I take it?" Dalila said.

Fargo nodded. "You're far enough away, it should be safe. Keep the animals quiet. No fire. You'll hear a lot of shooting and yelling but stay put." He gave the nun a pointed look. "That includes you."

"I thought you were leaving him but you're not."

"He has my sock," Fargo said.

"Why did you tie him to that tree?" Sister Angelina's face rippled. "Wait. I think I see. You're using Fermin as bait."

"He makes a good worm."

"Isn't there another way?"

Fargo nodded at the sisters. "Not if you want them to reach the convent alive." He turned. "Remember what I said. Stay put."

The slopes below the pass were empty of life but the bandits were there, somewhere. As he jogged back he looked for the telltale gleam of the spyglass.

Fermin Terreros was hunched over, red-faced, his chin slick with spittle and drops of vomit. His eyes were pools of hate.

Fargo hurriedly gathered firewood. The sun dipped and darkness crept over the valley. He arranged the logs in front of Terreros, who watched him with keen interest. A few stars sparkled as he kindled a flame.

Terreros made grunting noises, apparently hoping Fargo would remove the gag.

Fargo threw extra logs on the fire. "So they'll spot you from a long way off."

The bandit leader went into a paroxysm of rage. He uttered inarticulate noises. He gnashed his teeth. He tugged with all his might at the rope. It was in vain. When he was spent he lay on his side and glared.

"If looks kill could," Fargo said. He picked up the Henry and moved to where the finger blended into the forest. A log suited him but the log wasn't enough. He collected armfuls of fallen leaves and pine needles and dumped them next to it. Then, lying behind it, he pulled the leaves and needles over as much of him as they would cover. All he had to do to shoot was rise on his elbows. He willed the tension from his limbs and closed his eyes. It had been a long day and it was far from over.

Eighteen to one kept rolling through his mind. Formidable but not impossible odds, not if he handled it right. He didn't need to kill them all, only enough to persuade the rest he wasn't worth the bother. How many was enough depended on how loyal they were to Terreros.

Normally, bandit loyalties were skin-deep. A love of money and a lust for violence held them together. A weak glue, at best.

Night fell with a suddenness typical of the high country, and the meat eaters came to life. Howls and yips and snarls broke the tranquillity.

Fargo hoped the women did as he'd told them. If not, it was on their shoulders. He could protect them from the bandits. Protecting them from their own stupidity was something else entirely.

A commotion brought him out of his reverie. He rose and peered over the log.

Bathed in the firelight, Terreros was struggling mightily to free himself. His knees braced, he tugged and grunted and wrenched and grunted. The rope was thick; the knots were tight. All he did was tire himself out.

Fargo grinned. He went to lie back down, and froze. Something moved among the trees.

His first thought was that it must be another bandit but it was coming from down the valley, not up it. His second thought was that it must be an animal but few animals would approach so near the fire. A dreadful hunch gripped him, and he leaped up and over the log.

Sister Angelina was stooped over and taking small steps.

Her way of sneaking, Fargo reckoned, as he ran faster. She could ruin everything.

Fermin Terreros spotted her. He shifted and made noises, urging her on.

Fargo reached her as she reached the rope. Her fingers were clawing at a knot as he looped his arm around her waist and swept her off her feet. She was so thin and frail, she weighed next to nothing.

"No!" she bleated. "This isn't right!"

Terreros was beside himself with rage. He tried to butt Fargo in the leg but Fargo skipped aside and returned to the log. Sister Angelina fought him, pushing at his chest with her small hands and kicking her stick legs. He dumped her on her bottom and plopped down next to her.

"That was a damn stupid thing to do."

The nun looked at Terreros, covered her face with her hands, and wept. She cried without making a sound save for a few sniffles.

Fargo probed the woods and the grass. He supposed he should have expected this, and tied her, too. Now she had to stay there until it was over.

Her sniffling faded. She swiped a sleeve at her face and said softly, "I couldn't just do nothing."

"I told you that you still care for him."

"God help me, but yes, I do." Sister Angelina sank against the log. "After all these years, in defiance of all logic, despite what he is and what he has done, I care for him."

"I'm going to tell you something I've never told a nun before," Fargo said.

"What?" she asked, brightening slightly, apparently in the belief he would be sympathetic to her turmoil.

"You're a jackass."

Sister Angelina drew back. "Blunt, as always. And you are right. It is unforgivable. I have given my life to our Lord, and here I am, throwing all I believe in away to aid a man who is the devil incarnate." She bowed her head. "Life is so strange."

"Sister," Fargo said, propping his elbows on top of the log, "you don't know the half of it."

"I will go back with the girls." The nun rose halfway to her feet, her habit a tent on her spare frame.

"Like hell." Fargo grabbed her arm. "The bandits could be close."

"Or they could be high on the mountains. Dalila and Paloma will be worried. I should be with them."

"You should have thought of that sooner." Fargo patted the ground. "Have a seat."

"Please let me . . ."

From up the mountain, in the direction of the pass, a shot cracked. Just the one. The howls and other cries ceased and an unnatural quiet reigned.

"Was that a signal?" Sister Angelina whispered.

Fargo didn't know. The bandits were too savvy to give themselves away. Then again, they knew that he knew they were coming, so what did it matter?

Fermin Terreros swiveled toward the log, his face alight with glee, and laughed. He said something that was muffled by the sock.

"I think he said you are about to die," Sister Angelina mentioned.

"Wishful thinking."

High up, and faint, pebbles clattered. From up the valley came the *ching* of a hoof on rock.

"They are on their way."

Fargo wiped his palms on his buckskins. Eighteen to one went through his mind. What he wouldn't give to be back in Santa Fe in bed with Amalia.

"May I ask you something?" Sister Angelina said.

Fargo was in no mood to be distracted. "What?"

"Have you made your peace with our Maker?"

13

More rattling and clattering confirmed that some of the bandits were above the forest and descending. Sounds from up the valley warned him some were approaching from that direction, too. Then, across the creek, another shot cracked.

"We are surrounded," Sister Angelina whispered.

Not entirely, Fargo thought to himself. But the bandits hadn't done as he'd hoped and rushed in a pack to their leader's aid. They had wisely spread out and were converging on the fire from three sides. "Lie flat behind the log."

"You still intend to fight them?"

"It's them or us and I'll be damned if it will be us." Fargo raised the Henry to his shoulder. He still had an edge. The bandits had no idea where he was. Thanks to the fire, he could pick them off when they sought to free Terreros.

The bandit leader was trying furiously to free himself, and couldn't. He stopped and growled in frustration, then tried a new tack—he kicked at the fire in an effort to put it out but it was out of reach.

Fargo surveyed the night for movement. His peripheral vision registered motion where the finger of trees tapered near the stream. Two bandits were moving toward Terreros. Both wore sombreros and had rifles. They were not as cautious as they should be.

Terreros spotted them and gestured wildly and made gurgling sounds, trying to warn them. They kept coming.

Fargo frowned. His plan was unraveling. He'd hoped to lure in all of them at once. With the Henry's sixteen rounds, he could drop half before they could seek cover. Now if he shot these two, the rest would be harder to pick off.

Terreros had changed tactics again; he was frantically bob-bing his head toward the log, and gesturing with his bound arms.

The pair stopped. They were confused by their leader's an-tics. One said something and they came on again, more slowly.

Suddenly they stopped and stared hard. At him, Fargo thought, until he realized Sister Angelina had stood up and stepped over the log and was walking calmly toward them, her hands raised as if in benediction.

"I bid you stop what you are doing, in the name of the Lord. Forsake violence for the sake of your eternal souls."

Fargo was as astounded as the bandits. They looked at one another and the man on the right raised his rifle partway and lowered it again. He wasn't about to shoot a nun. The other bandit had no such compunctions; he took aim at Sister Angelina.

"Damn it," Fargo said under his breath, and cored the man's head from front to back. The second bandit fired at the Henry's muzzle flash. In return, Fargo put lead through the man's left eyeball.

Sister Angelina was almost to Terreros. She stopped and stood over him and made the sign of the cross.

From behind Fargo came the crash and crackle of under-brush. Spurred by the shots, the other bandits were coming on fast. Hurtling over the log, he ran to Sister Angelina and grabbed her elbow. "We have to get out of here!" He turned to flee down the valley.

A gun boomed, and lead chipped a tree branch.

Fargo fired at the shooter, only to have more guns boom from several directions at once.

Taking hold of Sister Angelina's waist, Fargo virtually carried her. She didn't resist. Once they were out of the ring of firelight the shooting tapered to a few stray blasts.

"I tried to stop the bloodshed," Sister Angelina said in his ear.

"They're killers," Fargo said.

"They are children of God, too."

"Get your head out of the clouds."

"Oh, senor."

Up the valley Yago hollered and was answered by a man

across the stream. The bandits were closing in a pincer on the finger and the fire.

"I do what I must," Sister Angelina said quietly. "I can't help being me."

"And they can't help being sons of bitches. Now hush up," Fargo said, and flew.

Dalila and Paloma were anxiously waiting. When Fargo burst from the dark and let go of the nun, they stifled outcries. Dalila ran over and threw her arms around him and pressed her cheek to his.

"I was so worried for you."

"What about me?" Sister Angelina asked with a hint of humor.

"And you too, Mother Superior, of course."

Paloma was listening to the night sounds. "Men are coming!" she whispered. "Do you not hear them?"

Fargo did. At least several of the bandits were uncomfortably near. "Mount up. Quickly." The sisters both turned to the dun and he whispered, "Paloma, you take the palomino."

"But that is Senor Terreros's horse."

"Take it anyway," Fargo said, and grinned at how mad Terreros would be. Swinging onto the Ovaro, he shoved the Henry into the scabbard. He rode slowly so as to make as little noise as possible but even a little was too much. Off in the night a man yelled and flame stabbed at them. Fargo answered with the Colt. Then they were at a trot, the women hemming the Ovaro in in order not to lose him.

They reached the lower end of the valley and Fargo stopped. The fire had been extinguished. By now Terreros had been untied and was fit to *be* tied. He would come after them with vengeance burning in his heart. But not until morning, Fargo reckoned. He clucked to the stallion and started up the next mountain. He wanted distance between them and the bandits. The climb was arduous. It took all the less than considerable skill the women possessed to keep up with him.

Sometime toward midnight, when they were high on a windswept ridge, Sister Angelina cleared her throat and announced, "I can't go on much farther, senor. I am worn out."

"Me too," Dalila said.

"We'll stop soon," Fargo promised.

In a "

kindling a

the nun wi

kets wrappe

"We are

dejectedly.

"It is worse

min when we t

she said "we" sh

redeem his honor.

It was perceptiv

be out for blood. Sp

"How far to the co

"We have strayed

Sister Angelina answer

"We won't make it."

"Chin up, child. The   as so
far, hasn't he?" Sister An   ne smile. "I
lost my senses for a while   I am myself again
and I have every confidence   or Fargo."

"The Lord or Fargo, which is it?" Paloma said.

"Perhaps one is the unwitting arm of the other."

Fargo snorted. "I like that unwitting part."

"I thought you would." Sister Angelina grew somber. "But
it has become a race with death for us. Fermin's rage will
know no bounds. He might not even spare me."

"There are two less," Fargo said.

"And there are four of us. You would do well to keep that
in mind. It is not on your shoulders alone."

"Us against the worst bunch of killers in the Southwest."
Fargo chuckled. "They don't stand a chance."

Dalila was wringing her hands. "Stop making light of it.
What do we do? How do we get out of this alive?"

"Maybe that God of hers will send a bolt out of the blue
and burn all the bandits to a cinder."

"Senor Fargo," Sister Angelina said.

"Is that all you can come up with?" Dalila said.

Unfortunately, at the moment, it was, Fargo admitted. They
talked a while more, and then the women turned in. Fargo
stayed up, drinking coffee and thinking. He needed to whit-

...he considered the
...ded to put the brain-

...ally broke, and Fargo roused
...ely. The sisters were eager to do
... the bandits; their virtue as well as
...ke. Sister Angelina quietly said she would
...uld but stressed that she wouldn't hurt any-

...es against all I believe. I am sorry but that is how it
...be."

Fargo nodded. He hadn't expected her to say different. She was who she was and wouldn't change.

Dalila didn't see it that way. "Those terrible men will do terrible things to my sister and me, and you don't care."

"I didn't say that."

"It is not the words, it is what you do, or in your case, what you won't do. I may be young but I'm not stupid. You are supposed to be so holy, to feel for everyone, but you use God as an excuse not to feel."

"Dalila!" Paloma said.

"It is true, sister, whether you agree or not. This sainted woman you think so highly of cares less for us than this man who is a stranger to our ways. He risks his life for us while she hides behind her vows."

"No more," Paloma said.

On that bitter note they fled. A fiery crest crowned the eastern horizon, blazing the mountains red and gold. It was half an hour before ants appeared on the valley floor far below, ants with sombreros and hats, and one of them holding a shiny brass tube that gleamed in the morning sun.

"They've seen us," Fargo said.

"Do you think they will guess what we are up to?" Dalila wondered.

"Even if they do, they won't stop."

"Pride," Sister Angelina said.

"That," Dalila responded, "and they want to rape and kill my sister and me."

They passed through dark ranks of closely spaced firs and stands of shimmering aspens. In a high meadow they startled

a cow elk and her calf. A pair of ravens kept them company for a while. They came across bear sign and the tracks of wolves and once the paw prints of one of the most elusive animals on the continent: a roving wolverine.

Then treacherous talus spread before them. Fargo reined to the right to go around.

Above the talus was a boulder field. Most of the boulders weren't any bigger than a breadbasket. One that was caught Fargo's eye. It was a quarter of the size of the Ovaro and teetered precipitously on an earthen lip near the talus. He rode behind it and drew rein.

"This will do."

"It must be heavy," Sister Angelina gauged.

"The four of us can move it," Fargo predicted.

"I pray you are right or the banditos will have us at their mercy."

The women rested while Fargo set to work. Drawing the toothpick, he dug at the dirt on the side of the boulder that faced down the slope. He exercised great care. If he dug too much away, the boulder would go crashing down. If he dug too little, the boulder wouldn't move when he wanted it to.

Sister Angelina sat near him.

"You want something?" Fargo asked between jabs of the toothpick.

"You're not the only one who has an idea how to end this. What would you say if I rode down the mountain to meet them?"

"I'd say you've been out in the sun too long."

"Hear me out," Sister Angelina urged. "Fermin still cares for me. You saw it for yourself. Why not use that against him?"

"You aim to beat him to death with your habit?"

"Gracious, no." Sister Angelina grinned. "I will get down on my knees and beg him to leave the rest of you be." She held up a hand when Fargo went to speak. "I know, I know. He's not likely to listen. But he might if I offer him the one thing in this world he would like to have more than you and the girls."

"What would that be?"

"Me."

Fargo stopped digging and looked at her.

"You heard him. He remembers how it was with us. He loved me back then and I suspect he still cares for me now."

"Not enough to spare us."

"There is only one way to find out, isn't there? I will go down to him and fall at his feet and plead."

"No." Fargo sat back. He had the lip as he wanted it. The rest was up to gravity.

"At my age I can do as I please, senor. Unless you are willing to tie me, you can't stop me."

"All right," Fargo said.

"All right, what? You won't try to stop me?"

"All right, I'll tie you."

"I never know when you are serious," she said.

The ants were the size of antelopes, and climbing rapidly. Bandoliers, gun belts, rifles and *pistolas*, gleamed. Yago was in the lead. Fermin Terreros was next. Now and again they stopped and passed the spyglass from one to the other. The next time that happened, Fargo waited for Yago to give the telescope to Terreros. He stood so Terreros could see him and held up his fist with his middle finger extended.

Terreros jerked the telescope down.

"You poke and you poke," Sister Angelina said.

Fargo had the women sit behind the boulder. He had done all he could. It would be an hour yet, maybe more, before the bandits caught up. Long enough for him to catch forty winks.

He laid on his side and rested his head on his arm.

"Senor Fargo?" Paloma said.

"I'm trying to sleep."

"How many banditos are left?"

"Sixteen, plus Terreros," Fargo said.

"There are no others?"

"Not that I know of." Fargo opened his eyes. "Why?"

"If all the banditos are below us, then who are they?" Paloma asked, and pointed across the valley.

Fargo raised his head. Seven riders were silhouetted on a far rim. At that distance the only detail he could make out was that they wore headbands. It was enough. "They're Apaches."

14

Skye Fargo smiled.

"You are happy to see them?" Sister Angelina said in surprise.

"I am if they take it into their heads to kill a few bandits."

"They could just as well take it into their heads to kill us."

"There's that," Fargo said. He couldn't tell which band the warriors belonged to.

Not that it mattered. *All* Apaches were hostile to whites, as they had been to the Mexicans before the whites and the Spanish before the Mexicans. And to most other tribes, as well. Whether those seven were Mescaleros or Chiricahuas or Jicarillas was irrelevant. "All we need now is for a grizzly to pop out of nowhere and our day will be complete."

Sister Angelina laughed. "Life is always full of surprises."

"Some I can do without." Fargo sat up and gazed down the mountain. Terreros and his men were still climbing. Across the valley, the Apaches watched. Their presence changed things. He hadn't said anything to the women but he'd intended to send them on ahead while he dealt with the bandits. Now he didn't dare. Apaches killed women as well as men. Sometimes a warrior took a white woman into his wickiup but it was rare. To the Apache, most white women were too weak or too shrewish to make good wives.

Fargo had to keep the nun and the sisters with him. It complicated matters. "Listen to me," he said to get their attention. "When the shooting starts, you're to stay flat on the ground. Don't get up for any reason."

"What if you are hurt?" Sister Angelina asked.

"Not for any reason whatsoever," Fargo stressed. If he was hit, if he went down, the women would have cause to envy him before their own ends came. He kept that to himself.

Drawing his Colt, he inserted a sixth cartridge. He levered a round into the Henry and made sure the Arkansas toothpick was in its ankle sheath.

"Girding for battle," Sister Angelina said.

Fargo turned to Dalila. "Where's that Smith and Wesson?"

"The what?"

"Terreros's revolver. I gave it to you. What did you do with it?"

"I put it in my saddlebag."

"Get it."

"I've never fired a gun in my life. I'm afraid I couldn't hit much unless a bandit was right in front of me."

"It's for me," Fargo said.

"Oh."

Fargo checked to see how many pills it had in the wheel: six. He jammed it under his belt next to his buckle. He sat and watched the bandits ascend. They were at the last belt of trees. In ten minutes or so they would reach the talus.

"Where did the Apaches go?" Paloma asked.

Fargo looked. The silhouettes were gone. There was no predicting what the warriors would do; they might go back to their village for more warriors, they might kill some of the banditos, they might come after him and the women.

The minutes crawled on tortoise feet. Fargo's throat was dry but he didn't touch the waterskin. They'd need every drop before this was over.

A sombrero-topped rider materialized at the edge of the talus. Then another and another. Fermin Terreros appeared, and Yago and Bartolo and the man called Slate. They drew rein.

"Here we go, ladies." Fargo moved behind the boulder and put his shoulder to it. The women followed suit. He dug in his boots and levered his legs, exerting every sinew in his body.

They pushed too.

The boulder didn't move.

"Uh-oh," Dalila said.

"Again." Fargo strained with all his strength and felt the boulder give slightly.

"Why won't it fall?" Paloma complained.

"One more time with all we've got," Fargo said.

The lip, weakened by his digging, gave way. The boulder lurched and tilted and tumbled, thumping the ground as it rolled end over end onto the talus. Below, the bandits were quick to awaken to the danger. Yago yelled, and they broke to the right and the left or fled back into the trees.

Dislodged by the boulder, the talus gained momentum. Tons of loose rock and stones and earth, rumbling as it moved, bore down on the scattering bandits.

Fargo had hoped to catch all of them in the brown avalanche, but a dozen, Terreros and Yago among them, were already in the clear.

One man's horse, for some reason, wouldn't move. He was flapping his legs and smacking its neck but it stood there as if made of wood and the next moment the talus was upon them. The horse squealed. The man screamed. Another bandit, his mount flying, was also caught. And a third. All were swept up like twigs and disappeared as if into shifting quicksand, the life crunched and crushed from their bodies in a hideous rending of flesh and bone.

"Only three," Fargo said. Sinking to a knee, he tucked the Henry's stock tight and steadied the barrel. A quick bead, and he fired at a bandit who had just escaped death.

He scored, too; the man flung out his arms and pitched from his saddle.

Fermin Terreros bellowed. Rifles and pistols cracked, unleashing a swarm of lead.

Fargo dropped flat. Prone, he fired as fast as he could work the lever. Another man toppled. Terreros bellowed again and the bandits raced for cover. Fargo sent lead after them but they were bent low over their saddles and many of them were weaving and he didn't drop any more.

"Damn." Fargo rose and darted to the Ovaro. "We're leaving, ladies." It wouldn't take the bandits long to reorganize. He held on to the Henry, and kicked. They climbed straight for the top. The mule lagged because of its age and Sister Angelina had to use her heels. They gained the summit without being shot at, and for all of five seconds Fargo was elated. Then he drew sharp rein, and swore.

"Oh my God," Dalila exclaimed.

They had come up one side of the mountain—only to find there was no "other side."

Instead of rolling slopes that would bring them to the next valley, they were on the brink of a precipice, a sheer cliff with a thousand-foot drop to jagged boulders. They had gone as far as they could go.

"What do we do?" Paloma cried.

Fargo reined around. Their only recourse was to go back down—into the gun sights of the waiting bandits.

"Think of something," Dalila said.

If it was dark Fargo would try to get past Terreros and his wolves. But in broad daylight, out in the open—they would be cut down before they reached the trees. "We'll make our stand here."

Dalila looked at him. "Are you loco?"

"We could throw ourselves on Fermin's mercy," Sister Angelina proposed.

"He doesn't have any," Fargo said.

"I would die before I let them touch me," Paloma declared. "I do not want a man between my legs, ever."

The bandits had dismounted and were fanning out along the tree line. Yago was using his spyglass.

"Climb down," Fargo said. His reins in hand, careful not to get too near the drop-off, he walked along the rim.

"What if the banditos shoot at us?" Dalila worried.

"We're out of rifle range." Fargo had a hunch Terreros wouldn't open fire even if they weren't. A bullet would be too easy. Terreros wanted them alive.

"I feel dizzy," Paloma said. She was peering over the rim.

"Then don't look down. Use your damn head." Fargo never had a problem with heights but even he felt a little queasy. Should any of them trip, or a horse or the mule misstep, they would plunge into oblivion.

Sister Angelina was much too near the edge. She had her head bowed and was muttering under her breath, her rosary clutched fast.

"What the hell are you doing?" Fargo demanded.

"Praying. What else?"

"Well, watch where you're going," Fargo snapped. "You're liable to go over."

"You shouldn't talk to the Mother Superior like that," Paloma scolded. "God will be mad at you."

"I thought He already was."

Sister Angelina stopped praying. "I know you jest, senor, but you must not blaspheme. Our Lord will forgive many things but never that."

"God," Fargo said.

Down below the talus, the bandits were leading their horses, keeping pace.

"What are they waiting for?" Dalila said. "Why don't they come get us?"

"The talus," Fargo said. Once it ended, that was exactly what the bandits would do.

He would have a choice to make. Go down fighting or let himself be taken.

"Be brave, Dalila," Sister Angelina said. "You too, Paloma. And don't listen to Senor Fargo. The Lord is not to blame for this."

"No," Dalila said. "You are."

"Excuse me?"

"I don't blame God. I blame you. This is all your fault. If you had listened to me and not our mother I wouldn't be in this predicament."

"Dalila," Paloma said.

"I don't care who she is or what she is," Dalila angrily replied. "I told her I didn't want to be a nun. I told her I did not want to go to the convent. But did she agree not to take me? No. She gave in to Mother and here I am."

"Here we are," Paloma said.

Fargo let them get it off their chests. It took their minds off the bandits, and what the bandits would do if they fell into their clutches.

"I am sorry you feel that way," Sister Angelina said.

Dalila snorted. "What good does that do us? We have been through hell and the worst is yet to come, and all you can say is that you are sorry?"

"I did what I thought best. If I had defied your mother and refused to bring you, she would have brought you to the convent herself."

The sisters didn't say anything.

"I knew your heart was not in it, Dalila," Sister Angelina went on. "I couldn't very well pretend to take you to the convent and let you go off on your own. It would be a betrayal of your mother's trust. So I did the next best thing I could think of. I hired Senor Fargo."

Fargo looked over his shoulder. "How the hell did I fit in?"

Sister Angelina grinned. "I was quite devious. I suppose I should be ashamed but I'm not. I was counting on you to save this poor girl from a fate she despised."

"I'm confused," Dalila said. "What exactly did you expect Senor Fargo to do besides take us to the convent?"

"I expected him to make love to you."

Dalila flushed red.

"You didn't!" Paloma exclaimed.

Fargo shook his head in disbelief. It was rare for anyone to shock him but this sure did.

"What the hell are you talking about?"

"Your language, senor, is atrocious." Sister Angelina's eyes were twinkling. "But it's simple, really. When I went to the *coronel* to ask about a man to help me, he mentioned that not only do you have a reputation as a fine scout, you also have a reputation for going to bed with everything in skirts."

"Sister Angelina!" Paloma bleated.

"Not everything," Fargo said.

"In fact, it was when the *coronel* mentioned your— What shall I call them? Exploits? It gave me the idea how to save Dalila."

"I still don't understand," Dalila said.

"Think, young one. What is one of the requirements of every young lady who aspires to join our order?" Sister Angelina didn't wait for her to answer. "The candidate must be pure. In other words, a virgin. Since Senor Fargo has seen to it that you're not, you will be free to go home. Your mother will be upset, naturally, but she won't hold it against you since she, herself, once wanted to be a nun and couldn't for the same reason."

"My mother?" Dalila was stupefied.

Sister Angelina nodded. "I know many secrets. Your mother could no more control her urges than you can."

Fargo was more interested in something else. "You knew we went off the other night? I thought you were sleeping."

"No. I was lying there praying you would live up to your reputation. When you went off, I snuck after you. Thankfully, you proved to be as randy as a goat."

Dalila was aghast. "You saw us?"

"I only watched for a little bit."

"Oh, Sister."

"It was all I could think of to do. I wanted to spare you, young one. A woman should not become a nun unless she wants it more than anything. I speak from experience."

"You wanted me to make love to him the whole time," Dalila marveled. "Why didn't you just say so?"

"Please. I had to be discreet. I am, after all, a woman of God."

"You'd make a good madam," Fargo said. "I know a whorehouse in Denver where you could get work."

Sister Angelina laughed.

Paloma was staring at all of them as if they were insane. "Am I the only one here who is pure in body and mind?"

"Don't look at me," Fargo said.

"Be at peace, child," the nun told her. "You will understand better when you are older."

"If I live to be a hundred I will still not think that a man and a woman lying together is right under any circumstances."

"Too bad your mother didn't feel that way," Fargo said.

Just then there was a bellow from down the mountain. The talus had come to an end and the bandits were climbing in a wide line, their rifles and pistols brandished. At the forefront strode Fermín Terreros. His expression and his posture radiated pure hate. "Gringo!" he yelled. "Raise your hands over your head or you and the *putas* die!"

"What do we do?" Paloma anxiously asked.

Fargo could make a fight of it but it would be suicide. At their backs was the precipice.

Cover was conspicuously absent. Outnumbered, and with the women to think of, he did the only thing he could—he reached for the sky.

15

The bandits were of mixed minds. Some passed bottles back and forth and laughed; they were in good spirits now that their quarry was caught. Others glowered and fingered their pistols and knives; they craved revenge for those who had been shot and crushed.

Terreros had led them down to the valley floor and made camp near the stream. The horses had been picketed. Slate and two other bandits had gone off into the forest and returned bearing a dead doe. A haunch was now roasting on a spit over a roaring fire.

Skye Fargo lay on his side, his wrists and ankles tied. He was surprised to still be breathing. Fermin Terreros had told the others that he wasn't to be harmed or they would answer to him.

Sister Angelina and the sisters were huddled together, the nun with her arms over their shoulders. The pale faces of Dalila and Paloma betrayed their fear.

Spurs jangled, and Yago squatted next to Fargo. Grinning, he poked Fargo in the side.

"It will not be long now, gringo. He is about ready to deal with you."

"He" being Terreros, who was sitting cross-legged by the fire and sucking down whiskey.

"Cat got your tongue, gringo? You can talk to me. I do not hate you as some of my friends do."

Fargo was tired of waiting for the ax to fall. "Why not?"

"Why don't I hate you? We are *bandidos*, senor. None of us should expect to die in bed. We kill and are killed in turn. It is the natural order of things, no?"

"Damned reasonable of you," Fargo said.

"No, senor. Practical. I learned long ago that there are things in life we cannot change. So why get mad over them, eh? Yes, you killed some of us. But if it had not been you, it would have been someone else. I will not get drunk over it or waste my time thinking up ways to kill you."

"Too bad your boss isn't practical," Fargo said.

"Oh, but he is. He will be sure to make you suffer before you die. The blood of our brothers demands it."

"What about their blood?" Fargo asked, with a nod at the women.

"The young ones will be dead by morning. All of us will have turns with them, and some are very rough." Yago paused. "As for the Mother Superior, she is special. Fermin has said that she will be taken to the convent and released."

"Damned decent of him," Fargo said.

"She tried to set him free, did she not? Fermin is many things, senor, many of them not very pleasant. But he never forgets a favor, and he is always loyal to those who are loyal to him. Believe it or not."

"Hard to," Fargo said.

"Ask him yourself, then. Here he comes."

Chugging from a bottle, Terreros swaggered over. His face was black and blue and swollen. The Smith & Wesson was back in his holster, and he had a hand on it. "Gringo," he said, and raised the bottle in mock salute. "It is time we talked."

"That's all?" Fargo said.

Terreros kicked him in the ribs.

The torment was excruciating. Fargo bit his lip to keep from giving the bastard the satisfaction of hearing him cry out. The waves of agony faded and he could breathe normally, if painfully.

"That tongue of yours," Terreros said, "will be the death of you yet." He chuckled and sank down, the bottle in his lap. "You must be wondering why I haven't killed you."

"You're like a cat with a mouse."

Terreros nodded. "And where is the fun in slaying a mouse the moment you have it in your mouth? Cats play with their prey, as I will play with you. Only later, after your arms and legs have been broken and your teeth have been pulled from your mouth will I stop playing and end it."

"I'll say one thing for you."

Terreros's chest swelled a little. "What would that be?"

"On my list of scum, you're near the top."

Terreros swore and raised a fist, and just as suddenly lowered it again. "No. I will not let you provoke me into losing my temper."

"Do we get to take part, jefe?" Yago asked.

"He is mine, and mine alone. He made me look the fool in your eyes and I must show you I'm not."

"We know that," Yago said. "We would not have lasted as long as we have if not for you. *Son muy inteligentes.*"

"Gracias," Terreros said, trying to act humble and not succeeding. He smirked at Fargo. "You see, gringo? My men think highly of me."

"Stupider always looks up to stupid," Fargo said.

Fermin Terreros bent toward him, his mouth twisted in a vicious slash. "I will tell you something in earnest, gringo. I have never wanted to kill *anyone* as much as I want to kill you."

None of them had noticed Sister Angelina come over. Dalila and Paloma were clinging to her habit as if they wanted to crawl under it.

"Pardon, Fermin, but I would have words with you."

"I told you to sit over there," Terreros said. "We will talk later."

"Now." The nun sat and Dalila and Paloma glued themselves to her back. "You owe me a favor and I would like to collect."

"I hope it is not what I think it will be."

"I tried to help you," Sister Angelina said. "I would have freed you if I could."

"For that I have spared you. What else would you have of me?"

"I would like you to also spare these two," Sister Angelina said, and put her arms around Dalila and Paloma.

"You ask too much," Yago said.

"I am talking to Fermin, not to you." Sister Angelina did not take her eyes off Terreros. "If you will not do it because I tried to help you, then do it because I meant something to you once."

"Once," Terreros said. "More years ago than these two have lived. But we are different people now."

"Please." Sister Angelina placed her hand on his knee. "Do this one good deed and I will be forever grateful."

"I do not want your gratitude," Terreros said. "I want only to be shed of you, and to never set eyes on you again."

"Oh, Fermin."

"Stop calling me that." Terreros shifted uncomfortably and tilted the bottle to his mouth. He gulped and said curtly, "I do not like that you appeal to my heart. Go sit where I told you and do not bother me again."

For such a small, unassuming woman, Sister Angelina was as tenacious as a bear. "I will not. These girls are in my charge. I must do all I can on their behalf."

"Keep this up and I will treat you the same as them."

A horse whinnied. Another stamped a hoof. Fargo craned his head to see why.

The Ovaro and several others had raised theirs and were gazing across the stream. The Ovaro pricked its ears. Something, or someone, was out there. "How do you feel about Apaches?" he asked.

Terreros tore his glare from Sister Angelina. "They are animals, or little better."

"They ever give you any trouble?"

"We have too many guns," Terreros said. "And we have two trackers who are part . . ." He stopped and his face hardened. "We *had* two trackers but you killed them. Why do you ask?"

"We saw seven Apaches earlier."

Terreros looked at Sister Angelina. "Is this true?"

"Yes, Fermin."

"Well, they won't bother us," Terreros said. "There are less of us thanks to your scout but we are still formidable."

"Better tell that to them," Fargo said.

"Eh?"

"An Apache is about to help himself to some of your horses."

The warrior was on his belly and almost to the string. He wore a headband and a breechclout and knee-high moccasins. Around his waist was a knife and a pistol.

Terreros spun and saw him and bellowed a warning. Like a bronzed scorpion, the Apache whirled and scuttled into the dark. A few shots were thrown after him as all of the bandits, Terreros included, dashed to their animals. Several ran after the Apache.

Fargo didn't waste an instant. Shifting, he hiked at his pants leg and thrust his fingers into his boot. He could just reach the toothpick. He tugged but it wouldn't come loose. The rope around his ankles was to blame. "Quick," he said to Sister Angelina. "Undo the knots on my legs."

She squatted and pried but her fingers were thin and her nails were short and the knots were tight. "It is hard."

"Let me help," Dalila offered.

Between the two of them they got the first knot undone.

The bandits were waiting for the men who had gone after the Apache to come back. Terreros, Yago, Bartolo and Slate were at the far end of the string, talking.

"Hurry," Fargo urged.

"We are trying our best," Sister Angelina said.

"Oh here," Paloma said, and bending, she snatched a burning brand from the fire and pressed it against the rope.

Sister Angelina and Dalila had to jump back or be burned.

Fargo felt intense heat and smelled an acrid odor. The rope parted, leaving a scorch mark on his boot. Paloma dropped the brand in the fire. Palming the toothpick, he cut the rope around his wrists.

One of the bandits had taken his Colt but his Henry lay on Terreros's blankets. Scooping it up, he backed away from the fire. "What are you waiting for, ladies?" he whispered.

"You have a plan?" Sister Angelina said.

"It's called running like hell."

In a knot they raced for the forest, the nun holding the hem of her habit so she wouldn't trip over it. Once they gained the woods, Fargo stopped and hunkered.

"What now?" From Dalila.

"Do we make for the convent or for Santa Fe?" Paloma asked.

Truth was, Fargo hadn't thought that far ahead. The important thing was to get away from the bandits. "I'm thinking," he stalled.

"You better keep us safe," Paloma said. "I want to be a nun, not be raped by bandits or Apaches."

"Keep your voice down, damn it," Fargo said. He moved off deeper into the trees, the three of them his shadows. They went a lot farther than he thought they would before an outcry warned him the bandits had discovered they were gone.

A short slope brought them to a wall of rock. It wasn't more than ten feet high and maybe twice that long. He bid the ladies sit while he leaned back and pondered.

"Is this your idea of escaping?" Paloma objected. "We need horses. We need guns. Why do you just sit there?"

"I'm admiring your body."

"Senor Fargo," Sister Angelina said, wagging a finger. "This is no time for you to play the goat."

"He can't help himself," Paloma said. "It is all men think about. Even my own father. My mother has often said it is a pity we cannot do without them."

"I would not want to," Dalila said.

"You are a hussy."

From the commotion at the camp, Fargo gathered that the bandits were saddling up to search for them. Terreros was doing a lot of yelling and sounded furious as hell. Fargo chuckled.

"What strikes you as funny now?" Sister Angelina asked.

"Your boyfriend is having a bad day."

Torches flared. At Terreros's command the bandits spread out, riding in twos and threes. The fiery blobs of light bobbed and waved with the movement of the riders.

"They will find us!" Paloma cried in alarm.

"Not if you keep your big mouth shut," Fargo said. "Everyone lie flat."

Several torches weaved among the trees. The riders went slowly. They were being cautious, as well they should with Apaches abroad. The torchlight played over their faces, and as they got closer, Fargo saw who they were: Yago, Bartolo and Slate. Yago was in the lead, sitting tall in the saddle, his sombrero tilted back on his curly thatch of hair.

Fargo tensed. If Yago came all the way to the rock wall, he and the women were as good as caught.

Twenty feet out the three men drew rein. Slate had a rifle. The other two had their hands on their pistols.

"No sign of them anywhere," Slate said.

"We better find them or Terreros will take it out on the rest of us," Bartolo glumly predicted. "He won't care that it's not our fault they got away."

"Fermin has not been himself since he saw the nun," Yago said. "She was once his woman, you know."

"That shriveled old prune?" Bartolo laughed. "Why did she turn to the cloth instead of staying with him?"

"You would have to ask her. He's never said and I'm not stupid enough to ask. You would be wise not to bring it up, either."

"I have no wish to die," Bartolo said.

"Do we keep looking or go back?" Slate asked.

"We go back when Terreros signals for us to go back and not before."

"I just don't like being out here with Apaches running around."

"Who does?" Yago said. "They are not like you and me. They can see in the dark like cats and . . ." He stiffened and peered to the north. "What's that?"

"I don't see anything," Slate said.

"I thought I did. Someone on foot."

"Let's keep looking," Bartolo advised. "We sit here like this, we make it easy for the Apaches."

"*Sí,*" Yago said, and gigged his mount—straight toward the rock wall, and Fargo and the women.

16

"Don't move," Fargo whispered. Darting to the end of the wall, he scrambled to the top and moved back along it until he was above the women.

Yago was almost there. He had his torch over his head and was peering into the dark. Bartolo and Slate trailed after him.

Fargo didn't shoot. It would bring the rest of the bandits. He coiled, and when Yago came around the last tree and the light splashed over Sister Angelina and the girls, he vaulted out and down. Yago was focused on the women. He looked up just as Fargo slammed into him. Fargo smashed the Henry's stock against Yago's head as he struck, and they both tumbled, Yago to fall flat and lie still, Fargo to roll up into a crouch with the Henry pointed at Bartolo and Slate, who had drawn rein in surprise and were reaching for their pistols.

"Touch them and you're dead."

Slate froze.

Bartolo hesitated, then jerked both his hands in the air. "You are the one who is a dead man, gringo. Terreros will have you staked out and your skin peeled from your body."

"He has to catch me first." Fargo stepped closer. "Climb down."

"Damn you to hell," Slate said, but he obeyed.

Again Bartolo hesitated. "Shoot us and our friends will be on you like mad bees and gun you down."

"Maybe so," Fargo allowed, "but you won't be around to see it." He trained the Henry on Bartolo's swarthy face.

"Very well, gringo." Bartolo's saddle creaked and he planted both boots flat and elevated his arms. "But know this. If Terreros doesn't kill you, I will."

"Is that a fact?" Fargo rammed the stock against his ear

and Bartolo folded at the knees. He pointed the rifle at Slate. "How about you? Anything to say?"

"I never argue with a gent holding a gun on me."

"Smart," Fargo said, and drove the muzzle into Slate's gut. Slate doubled, and Fargo brought the stock down hard on the back of his head. Slate's torch fell and lay sputtering like the others.

"What are you waiting for?" Fargo said to the women. "Pick a horse and get on."

Sister Angelina moved to Slate's horse, saying, "You are brutal, senor."

"Better brutal than dead." Fargo helped her mount. The sisters climbed on Bartolo's animal, leaving Yago's for him. Before he forked leather he helped himself to Yago's Colt and jammed it into his holster.

"Aren't you forgetting something?" Paloma said.

"Guns for you?" Since they couldn't shoot worth a damn, Fargo didn't think it necessary.

"No, them." Paloma nodded at the sprawled forms. "You have a knife. Slit their throats before they come around."

"Paloma," Sister Angelina said.

"It is common sense. If he doesn't they will come after us."

She had a point, Fargo conceded, but he wasn't a cold-blooded killer. He didn't shoot men when their backs were turned, or when they were asleep, or unconscious.

"And you want to join the Sisters of Apostolic Grace?" Sister Angelina chided. "You must learn compassion, child."

"Compassion is a worthy trait," Paloma said, "but not if it gets you killed." She appealed to Fargo. "Tell her it is a mistake to let them go on breathing."

"It's a mistake," Fargo said.

"Then you will do it?"

"No."

"Why?"

Fargo pointed. Torches blazed about in the woods. Other bandits were straying in their direction. He pricked his spurs to the horse and the dark enveloped them. There was no moon, which worked in their favor.

Fargo's main concern was to get the woman to safety. But in all that vast wilderness the only haven was the convent, which was days away even if they rode their mounts into the ground. Or they could head back to Santa Fe but that was even farther.

They were caught between a rock and a hard place, the rock being the banditos and the hard place being the Apaches, with no help to be had other than their own wits.

Then there was the matter of the Ovaro and his Colt. He would be damned if he would let the bandits keep them.

Something moved higher up the slope.

Fargo drew rein and brought the Henry to bear. Whatever it was, it was gone. He'd caught only a glimpse and it might have been an animal.

"Why have we stopped?" Dalila whispered.

"Be quiet." Fargo would swear that unseen eyes were on them. Not Apache eyes, he hoped, and rode on.

A pair of torches were moving along the stream. Others seemed to float through the air on the other side of the valley.

An owl hooted. To the north a mountain lion screamed.

Fargo neared the end of the valley below the pass. To attempt to climb at night would be foolhardy. The women were poor riders. He remembered seeing a knoll that stood apart from the timber but was covered with pines. It would be as good a spot as any to wait out the night.

The torches were congregating near the bandit camp. Evidently Terreros had called off the hunt.

Fargo rode a little faster. He spooked a small animal. A raccoon, he thought, although all he saw was a bushy tail.

A short climb brought them to the knoll. The pines were thick except in the center.

Sister Angelina was the last to ride up. She was bent over in her saddle, her head hanging.

"Here," Fargo said, and helped her down. She was light as a feather and as frail as a twig. Sagging against him, she put her forehead on his chest.

"*Gracias*, Senor Fargo."

"Are you all right?"

"Perfectly fine."

Paloma spread blankets while Dalila fussed with her hair. It was the latter who said, "Tell him the truth, Mother Superior. If you don't, I will."

"Now, now," Sister Angelina replied. Taking a step back,

she clasped her hands and smiled. "Pay no attention to her, senor. She worries needlessly."

"Tell him about the pains," Dalila insisted.

"They are nothing," the nun said. "I am not as young as I once was. All this activity tires me."

Dalila turned to Fargo. "She confided in me last night. I woke up and she was holding her side and groaning. I wanted to wake you but she wouldn't let me."

"What pains?" Fargo asked.

Sister Angelina acted embarrassed. "They are nothing, I tell you. I've had them for a while now. A month or so. They come and they go. Here." She pointed at her garment on her right side. "It is just a stomach upset."

"You didn't go to a doctor while you were in Santa Fe?"

"Doctors cost money. Besides, I have faith that the Lord will not have me die before my time."

"You're having the pain now?" Fargo asked, and when she nodded, he pressed his hand where she had pointed. She gasped and doubled over and would have fallen had he not caught her. Gently, he carried her to a pine and sat her down with her back to the trunk.

"Sorry," she said weakly. "You caught me by surprise."

"Stomach upset, my ass," Fargo said.

"For the last time, please watch that tongue of yours."

Dalila and Paloma had rushed over. Dalila tenderly touched the old woman's wrinkled cheek.

"I may not want to be a nun but I still hold you in high regard. Is there anything I can do?"

"No, my dear," Sister Angelina said. She patted Dalila's hand. "Why don't you and your sister lie down and get some sleep? We have another grueling day ahead of us tomorrow, I'm afraid."

"I'd rather stay with you," Paloma offered.

"Please. I am perfectly all right."

Fargo held his peace until the girls were covered to their chins. Then he whispered, "I want the truth. How long have you really had the pains?"

"About a year," Sister Angelina confessed.

"You must have some idea what's wrong," Fargo said. Nuns ministered to the sick a lot, and knew a lot about illness.

"I think I have a cancer."

"Hell," Fargo said.

"Don't tell them. The girls would fuss over me and I'm not helpless yet." Sister Angelina wearily closed her eyes. "I am sorry to be a burden."

"Do you hear me complaining?"

"No, but you wouldn't. You act tough and you don't take, what is the white word, guff? But you have a good heart whether you admit it to yourself or not."

"You have me all figured out."

Sister Angelina chuckled. "I have lived a long time, senor. I have learned to see people as they are and not as they pretend to be."

"You sure had me fooled."

"Pardon?"

"Terreros. He's a mean son of a bitch. He doesn't care about anyone but him. Yet you keep appealing to the good nature he doesn't have."

Sister Angelina looked away. "I should think I know him better than you."

"And then there's me," Fargo said. "I like whiskey. I like a game of cards. I like whores. Some folks wouldn't call that being good."

"I spoke of your heart, senor. You could abandon us and save yourself but you don't. Is that not the mark of a good man?"

"I gave my word," Fargo said. "Just as I'm giving you my word now that before this is over, that son of a bitch you think so highly of will burn in hell."

"Oh, senor."

Fargo got Yago's bedroll and spread it out for her. "This should keep you warm. We can't risk a fire."

"I understand."

Fargo walked to the valley side of the knoll and sat with the Henry across his legs. The only light anywhere was the glow of the bandit campfire. The night was still save for periodic gusts. The wolves, the coyotes, the owls were quiet. He tiredly rubbed his eyes and wished he could heat coffee to keep him awake. He yawned, and shook himself.

The stars were molasses in their nightly orbits.

Suddenly footfalls padded. Fargo swung around and caught a suggestion of long hair and the rustle of a dress. "What are you doing up?"

"I couldn't sleep," Dalila said. She sat next to him. "I thought you wouldn't mind company."

"Your sister and Angelina?"

"Sound asleep." Dalila fluffed her hair. "I am worried about the Mother Superior. What will we do if she dies?"

"Bury her."

"We should take her to the convent."

"Pack her body all that way?" Fargo shook his head. "She'll be ripe long before we get there."

Dalila leaned back so that her breasts bulged and then rubbed her arms. "It is chilly, is it not?"

"I'm fine," Fargo said. Out of the corner of his eye he saw her frown.

"What can I do to keep warm?"

"The first bear we see, I'll shoot it and skin it and make you a fur coat."

Dalila did more rubbing. She was watching to see if he noticed and when he didn't react, her frown deepened. "It is a shame men are so thickheaded."

"What was that?" Fargo said. "I wasn't paying attention."

"We are safe here, are we not?" Dalila asked.

"As safe as we can be anywhere in these mountains," Fargo answered. Which, when he thought about it, wasn't safe at all.

"The bandits do not know where we are, yes?"

Fargo grunted.

"The others are asleep, yes?"

Fargo grunted again.

"I have given you hints and you sit there like a bump on a log and make pig noises at me."

"Oink," Fargo said.

"You are not nearly as funny as you think you are. It would serve you right if I got up and left."

Fargo didn't take his eyes off the woods. He was bothered by the thing he saw earlier. It could have been a deer—or it could have been an Apache. Most people believed, with good reason, that Apaches rarely attacked at night. While it was true they didn't like to, they still would when it suited them.

"Are you even listening to me?"

"I'm trying not to."

"How can you sit there and insult me after I have given myself to you? Have you no decency?"

"Not a lick," Fargo said.

Dalila was growing mad. She slid around in front of him so he had to look at her, and put her hands on her hips. Her breasts appeared to be trying to climb out of her dress. "You know what I want."

"Tacos?"

"It will help me sleep."

"So will a conk on the head."

"Yes or no," Dalila demanded.

"Since you put it that way." Fargo reached out with both hands and placed them on her mounds.

"Oh my," Dalila said huskily. "You've been playing with me this whole time, haven't you?"

"You think so?"

Fargo squeezed, hard. Dalila glued her mouth to his and her tongue probed his lips.

She was panting through her nose and they had hardly begun. He kneaded her breasts and sucked on her tongue while around them the valley lay peaceful under the myriad of stars.

"I've wanted you so much," Dalila whispered when they broke for breath. "I can't stop thinking about the last time."

Fargo nipped her earlobe.

Unexpectedly, Dalila drew back. "Did it surprise you, Sister Angelina wanting you to make love to me? It surprised me. But now I do not need to be a nun, thanks to her."

"I helped," Fargo said, running a hand down her thigh.

"Sí. But I think you would help Paloma, too, if she were willing, and any other woman in New Mexico."

"That's me," Fargo joked. "A heart as big as the whole territory."

"It is not your heart that is big, senor," Dalila said, and placed her fingers on his manhood. "It is this magnificent pole of yours. You are a stallion."

"How would you know? I'm your first."

"A girl hears things. And she spies when she can."

"You watched your own folks?" Fargo would have laughed except it might wake the others.

Dalila shrugged. "I was curious, and much younger." She rubbed him through his pants. "When I touch you, my blood grows hot. It is a good feeling."

Fargo bent his mouth to hers to shut her up. He pulled her onto his lap and she parted her legs and straddled him. Face-to-face, they kissed and caressed while he undid her dress. Her breasts were gorgeous; round and full and peaked by twin tacks. He cupped one and inhaled it and swirled the nipple. She pulled him hard against her and knocked off his hat running her fingers through his hair.

"Ohhhhh, yes. I like that."

Fargo cupped the other breast. She rubbed against his leg, her hips rocking. A dreamy expression came over her, and she moaned.

"I could do this forever."

Not Fargo. Not with Apaches out there somewhere. He slid her dress up around her waist and freed his member, then stiffened when she wrapped her warm hands around him and commenced to lightly stroke.

"Magnífico!" she breathed.

Fargo grit his teeth and barely kept from exploding. She would have gone on stroking but he moved her hands and raised her off his lap. The tip of his manhood brushed her nether slit. She sensed what he was going to do and gripped his shoulders.

"Yes," she said.

Fargo rammed up into her. Her velvet sheath quivered and her whole body shook and she sank her teeth into his upper arm and then grinned devilishly.

"It feels so good."

Fargo began to thrust and she put her feet flat and pumped her legs to match the pace he set. Up and down, in and almost out, over and over. A part of Fargo stayed alert to the night sounds that might forewarn of a slinking enemy.

Voicing tiny moans of pleasure, Dalila pumped harder. Her eyes were closed, her rosy lips parted. The tip of her tongue stuck out.

Fargo couldn't say what made him look over his shoulder.

A sense, maybe, that they were being watched. He glanced around, and there was Paloma, not ten feet away. Her face was in shadow. The moment he turned, she whirled and bolted.

Dalila didn't see her. Eyes still shut, she was at the apex of release. She ground against him almost violently, arched her body, and gushed.

"Ahhhhhhhh!"

Fargo felt her tighten, felt the wet, and a keg of black powder exploded below his waist. He humped off the grass, battering her with his ram, the slaps of their bodies muffled by the folds of her dress. Eventually they subsided and she collapsed against his chest, completely spent.

"I could do that every night."

So could Fargo. He groped at his side, found his hat, and jammed it back on. "You should go back."

"In a minute." Dalila kissed his chin and his cheek and his mouth. "You'll always be special."

"Special?" Fargo repeated. He was thinking of Paloma. It was best, he decided, not to tell Dalila.

"You are my first," she said, and traced his jaw with her fingertip. "The first one is always special, no?"

"For some," Fargo said.

"Have you no romance in your soul?" Dalila teased. She slid off and set to rearranging her clothes.

Fargo patted his holster to be sure the revolver hadn't fallen out from all the bouncing, and pulled at his pants. "We need to talk."

"About us?"

"About Angelina. She needs a doc. We should forget about the convent and take her to Santa Fe."

"I have no objection. I never wanted to go to the convent in the first place. But she won't agree."

"I'll tie her on her mule and take her anyway." Fargo had another reason for turning back. Terreros expected them to try for the convent and would ride to head them off. By the time the bandit leader realized they had tricked him, it would be too late to stop them.

"She will be mad," Dalila said.

"Better mad than dead." Fargo grasped her wrist. "I can count on you to back me on this?"

"*Sí*, senor. I have always had great affection for the Mother Superior. I have even more now that I have learned what she did to spare me from spending the rest of my life miserable."

Dalila smoothed her dress. "If you need me to keep watch, come wake me. I will be happy to take a turn." She blew him a kiss and walked off.

Down the valley the bandit campfire still flickered. Fargo figured they would keep it going all night as a precaution against the Apaches. Not that it would help much. Apaches were ghosts when they wanted to be.

No sooner did the thought cross Fargo's mind than an iron arm looped around his neck from behind and clamped onto his throat. At the same instant, a blade glinted in the starlight.

He got his arm up to block it and seized the warrior's wrist. A knee slammed into his back, racking him with torment, and he was shoved toward the ground. He went with it, tucking into a roll, and flipped his attacker over his shoulder.

Twisting in midair, the warrior landed on his feet. For a few heartbeats they stared at one another.

Fargo's right hand was in his boot. He swept the toothpick out just as the Apache lunged. Dodging, he slashed the warrior's arm and the Apache sprang back. They circled, seeking an opening. Fargo feinted and backpedaled to avoid a counterthrust. He speared the toothpick at the warrior's face but the man twisted aside. Fargo did it again and the Apache twisted in the same direction. Expecting it, Fargo planted a boot. The blow knocked the warrior back but he stayed on his feet. Deadly quick, the Apache stabbed at Fargo's middle. Fargo spared himself by the width of a whisker and cut at the Apache's jugular. He felt the knife sink into flesh. Before he could close in and finish it, the warrior wheeled and sped down the knoll with a hand pressed to his neck.

Fargo didn't go after him. It could be a trick. Or it could be the Apache was going to find another Apache to treat the wound. Apaches were fierce fighters but they weren't fools. They never threw their lives away if they could help it.

Of more concern were the warrior's friends. Wheeling, Fargo ran to where the women lay. He regretted having to wake them. They were worn out. Sister Angelina was on the verge of exhaustion. He stepped to Dalila and bent and saw that her eyes were open and that she was grinning.

"Have you come to do it again?" she asked.

"Apaches. Get your sister up." Fargo went to the nun. Her wrinkled face was smooth in repose, making her look twenty years younger. He hesitated, then gently shook her. She didn't stir. He shook again, a little harder. Her eyelids fluttered and she mumbled in her sleep. "Angelina. You need to wake up."

She was slow doing so. Rising on her elbows, she gazed about in confusion. "*¿Quién es?*"

"Fargo," he answered. "The Apaches know where we are. We have to make ourselves scarce and we have to do it now."

"Apaches?" Sister Angelina looked toward the horses and then at the sisters. "Oh. Now I remember. I'm not at the convent, am I?"

"Let me help you." Fargo slipped a hand under her arm.

"*Por favor*, a moment," Sister Angelina said. "I feel lightheaded. I do not have my wits about me."

Fargo waited but his nerves jangled. He had barely held off one Apache; he sure as hell couldn't hold off seven.

"I was having the most pleasant dream. I was young, and with Fermin, and he and I were happily married. We were going to have a baby and I was so happy."

"That's nice," Fargo said. He was listening for the pad of moccasins.

"That is the one thing I most missed when I was a novitiate," Sister Angelina said. "I had always wanted children." She put a hand to her forehead. "I have seldom had a dream so real."

"The Apaches," Fargo said again.

"*Sí, sí, comprendo*. We must be on our way."

Fargo carefully raised her off the ground. He was appalled at how weak she was. She had to lean against him for a bit before she could take her first step. "How bad off are you?"

"I am fine."

"Bullshit."

Sister Angelina waggled a finger. "Have you lived so long on the frontier that you have forgotten how to behave in the presence of a lady?" She took several halting steps toward their animals. "My legs do not seem to want to do as they should."

"We have no time for this," Fargo said, and sweeping her up, he carried her to the horse and deposited her astride its back. "Are you fit enough to ride?"

"I will do what I must. You can count on me."

Fargo reined toward the high pass. With a little luck they would be over it by morning. But it was slow going. They had gone about a quarter of a mile when hooves clattered and someone was next to him. "What do you want?"

"I would have words with you, senor," Paloma said.

"Now?" Fargo said. She'd hardly spoken to him the whole journey. "Can't it wait until daylight?"

"No, senor, it cannot. My sister tells me you do not intend to take us to the convent. She says we are going back to Santa Fe."

"So?"

"So you did not ask my opinion and in my opinion it is a mistake. The Mother Superior wants to go to the convent. I want to go to the convent. You were hired to take us to the convent and that is what you should do."

"Aren't you forgetting the bandits and the Apaches?"

"I forget nothing. But the Apaches do not bother the nuns. I imagine it is only you they want to kill."

Fargo wondered if she realized what she was saying. "You don't give a damn if I'm dead?"

"No, senor. Not even a little damn. Remember, I saw you with my sister. I know you for what you are."

"And what would that be?"

"You are a typical man, senor. That is to say, you are a pig. To you a woman is good for one thing. Two things, if you count cooking to fill your pig bellies."

"Don't beat around the bush," Fargo said. "Give it to me straight."

Paloma ignored his taunt. "My sister doesn't mind that men are pigs but I do. I never want to marry. I never want to so much as be touched by one of you. I would rather be dead than be defiled."

"Your mother must have liked it."

"You mock me, senor. But I think no more highly of her than I do of you. My mother is a cow. She is slow and stupid and picked a man as stupid as she is."

"She know how highly you think of her?"

"The only good thing my mother has ever done is to arrange for me to become a nun. Once I am behind the convent walls, I can say good-bye to her and all the men in this world and be happy at last."

"Speaking for the men," Fargo said, "we won't miss you."

"Again you belittle me. But we have strayed off the subject. I demand you turn around and take us to the convent."

Fargo chuckled.

"I fail to see the humor, senor. I am most serious."

Fargo had met her kind before, people so full of themselves, they didn't give a lick about anyone else. "You want to go to the convent, be my guest. The rest of us are heading for Santa Fe."

"I can't seem to make you understand how important it is to me. To be a nun has long been my dream. Since I was little I have imagined how wonderful it will be."

"Good for you."

"You are too frivolous, senor. What must I do to make you see that I will not let you or anyone else stand in my way?"

"Should I be scared?"

"You are making a mistake," Paloma warned. "I want to go and I *will* go, and the Mother Superior will go with me."

Fargo's patience was at an end. "No way in hell, little girl. Now clam up and get back in line."

Paloma slowed to fall behind him, saying, "Very well. Don't say I didn't warn you. I am not weak like my sister. From here on out, as you gringos say, you would do well to watch your back."

Just what Fargo needed.

17

They made it to the pass but not by sunup.

Sister Angelina collapsed as they were climbing through the last of the timber. Dalila hollered Fargo's name and he reined around to find the nun on the ground. She had fallen off her horse. He hurried to help her. She couldn't stand without aid, and wasn't strong enough to ride on her own. He gave the horse's reins to Paloma and rode double with Sister Angelina, her in front, him behind holding her on.

Once out of the trees the slopes were open. The pass was half a mile above. Fargo tried not to think of Yago and his spyglass. All he could do was mentally cross his fingers.

Sister Angelina had slumped forward but now she roused and raised her head and said softly, "I am sorry, senor, to be such a burden."

"You're light as a feather," Fargo said.

"That's not what I meant and you know it." Sister Angelina turned her head and gave him her serene smile. "You've been a godsend."

"Godsend *and* a randy goat? That takes some doing."

Sister Angelina chuckled, and coughed. "Please do not make me laugh. It hurts when I do."

She sobered and clasped his sleeve. "No matter what happens to me, do I have your word that you will get Paloma to the convent?"

"She's determined to get there."

"Your word, Senor Fargo? I have learned many things about you since we met, and one of them is that you never break it."

"I'll get her there if she lets me," Fargo said. "And Dalila?"

"You already know the answer. She must return home. I

wish I could talk to her mother and explain so her mother won't be spiteful but I won't live that long."

"You never know," Fargo said.

"Yes," Sister Angelina responded, "I do."

After that they didn't talk until they reached the pass. Fargo carefully placed Sister Angelina on a blanket. She closed her eyes and was immediately out.

Paloma, downcast, was at his elbow. "How bad is she?"

"Bad," Fargo said.

"This is your fault. If you had eluded the banditos and the Apaches, she would not have worn herself out."

"Want to blame me for winter, too?"

Paloma's feelings toward him were as flinty as the hard glint to her eyes. "You're saying it couldn't be helped. That you have done the best you can. But your best hasn't been good enough, has it? And now the sweetest woman in the world will die."

"And the biggest bitch will become a nun," Fargo said.

"I hate you, senor."

"I'll try not to lose sleep over it." Fargo walked to where he could gaze down the mountain at the valley. Dalila was already there. A line of riders were filing up the lowest slope. Even at that distance he could see that the last of them was leading the Ovaro.

"They saw us, didn't they?" Dalila said forlornly.

"Yes."

"What now? Do we ride for our lives? Sister Angelina wouldn't last long."

"We stay here for as long as she lasts."

"Can you fight them off?"

"I'll sure as hell try." Fargo had rounds left in the Henry, and Yago's Colt. The rest of his ammunition was in his saddlebags so he would have to make each shot tell. He also had the advantage of the open ground between the timber and the pass.

"I will make coffee," Dalila said. "I found some in the saddlebags on the bandito's horse."

"With rocks for firewood?"

"I have a surprise for you."

She had thrown everything except the coffee out of the

saddlebags, and as they were climbing through the trees, she'd broken off low limbs and jammed them in the saddlebags to use later. "I was thinking ahead. I did good, yes?"

"You did real good."

"There is a canteen on the palomino. My sister told me it is half full. Can we use it or must we save it?"

"Make the coffee," Fargo said. He needed it to help stay awake.

After that there was little to do but sit and wait. Fargo went through the saddlebags on the other two horses and discovered cartridges for the Colt.

The aroma of the coffee roused Sister Angelina. She asked Dalila's help in sitting up and sat sipping quietly. The sisters hovered by her, eager to attend to her every need.

Fargo perched on a flat boulder watching the bandits. It would be hours yet before they reached the pass. A long notch high atop a mountain, it was about a hundred feet from end to end.

"Senor Fargo!" Dalila called. "Mother Superior would like to speak to us."

The nun's complexion reminded Fargo of a bedsheet. She patted the ground and he sat and she took his hand in both of hers.

"We never know the time or place, do we? I always thought it would be in my bed with the other Sisters around me." Angelina gazed longingly in the direction of the faraway convent, and sighed. "But enough of that. I have a few things to say to each of you. Dalila, be patient with your mother. She will come to understand this was for the best but it might take her a while. Paloma, be the best nun you can be. Don't be so judgmental of others. Thou shalt not judge, remember?" She raised Fargo's hand to her lips, and kissed it. "*Gracias*, senor, for all you have done, and all you will yet do. I am sorry I cannot see this through."

"Don't talk like that," Dalila said. "You're not dead, yet."

"Yes, child," Sister Angelina replied softly. "I am." She smiled and closed her eyes and sagged.

Fargo held her. He felt her wrist for a pulse and shook his head. Dalila sobbed. Paloma got up, turned her back on them, and moved off, her body rigid. Fargo laid Sister Angelina down and folded her hands on her chest. He didn't have anything to dig with so he gathered rocks, big rocks, small rocks, every rock he could find, and covered her. He was almost done when Paloma came back.

"What is this, you fool? Take those off her. We must put her on her mule and get her body to the convent."

"We'll come back for it later," Fargo said. He didn't add, "Provided we live long enough."

"Come back?" Paloma said. "We're going somewhere?"

Fargo nodded. "We're riding like hell for Santa Fe." They had enough of a lead on the bandits that he was confident he could get the girls to safety.

"But you said you were going to make a fight of it here," Paloma said. "Your very words."

"That was when I had Sister Angelina to protect," Fargo patiently explained. "Now that she's gone we can go."

"And leave her body untended? I won't permit that."

"You don't have any damn say. We head out in two minutes." Fargo went to the overlook to check on the bandits. The sun glinted off what might be Yago's spyglass, and he raised an arm and waved. Suddenly there was a sharp yell from the pass, and the pound of hooves. He whirled. Two of the horses were already in flight and Paloma was smacking a rock against the last's flank. She hit it so hard she drew blood, and the startled horse galloped off.

"What the hell?" Fargo blurted, and ran toward her.

Paloma threw the rock after the horses and cackled with glee.

In a fury, Fargo seized her wrist and shook her and she laughed in his face. It was rare for him to hit a woman but he came close to hitting her. He shoved, and she sprawled at his feet.

Disbelief writ on her features, Dalila rushed over. "God in heaven, sister! What have you done?"

"I told him!" Paloma crowed. "I told him we can't abandon her."

"Mother Superior is *dead*," Dalila cried.

"We can't abandon her body. Don't you see? We must do

all we can to safeguard it." Paloma jabbed a finger at Fargo. "He wanted to go off and leave her. Now he can't. Now he must stay and protect her the same as if she were alive."

"No, no, no," Dalila said, staring in horror at the horses as they disappeared out the far end of the notch. "They were our only hope."

Fargo was struggling to control his temper. The girl had put him in the worst possible situation.

"Trust in God," Paloma was saying as she rose and swatted dust from her dress. "That is what Mother Superior would say."

"You pitiful fool," Dalila said.

"No need to be insulting." Paloma drew herself up to her full height. "But then, I keep forgetting you didn't think as highly of her as I did."

"That's a lie."

"Is it? Which one of us will spend the rest of her days as a Sister of Apostolic Grace? And which of us ruined her chance by parting her legs for this disgusting gringo?"

Fargo slugged her. He held back, not because he wanted to but because if he hit her with all his strength he would have broken her jaw and shattered her teeth. She went down like a poled cow, in a heap.

"Oh, senor," Dalila said.

"She had it coming."

"For many years, yes. She has always been like this. She does what she wishes and the rest of the world be damned." Dalila stooped and tenderly touched Paloma's cheek. "But she is still *mi hermana pequeña*, my littler sister, and I love her."

Fargo jogged toward the end of the pass. He had a hunch what he would find and his hunch proved right; the horses were well down the other side of the mountain and showed no sign of stopping anytime soon. "Damn her," he said, and started back.

The extra ammunition for the Colt was gone. All he had were the cartridges around his waist. That wouldn't stop the bandits for long once the Henry went empty. If he was really the bastard Paloma thought, he'd chuck her off a cliff. The only consolation, and it was no consolation at all, was that she had put herself in the same danger. If the bandits got their hands on her, she would suffer dearly for her mistake. "Damn her," he said again.

Paloma was still out. Fargo stepped over her and went to see how high Fermin Terreros and company had climbed. They were pushing their mounts. By noon they would be within rifle range.

Dalila was glumly regarding the banditos. "I take it our horses, as you gringos say, are long gone?"

"Thank your sister," Fargo said.

"For a short time I dared to hope we would make it out of this nightmare alive," Dalila said. "Now I know better."

"You never know." Fargo chose a suitable boulder and wearily sank down.

"They have many rifles and *pistolas*."

"Don't remind me."

"Is there anything I can do?"

"If your sister comes around, hit her with a rock."

Dalila laughed but there was no mirth in it. "I should have watched her more closely. She has always been unpredictable. When she was little she caused a lot of trouble for our parents. Once she beat a cat to death for peeing on her blanket. Another time my mother slapped her and she slapped my mother back."

"A nun in the making," Fargo said.

"You are too *cínico*, yes? Cynical—is that the word?"

"You should leave," Fargo said. "Down the other side of the mountain. In case they get past me."

"We both know I wouldn't get far, as tired as I am. Then there is Paloma. She won't leave Mother Superior."

"Forget her. You're more important."

Dalila smiled. "What a sweet thing to say. But I couldn't live with myself. I must stay as much for her as for you." She glanced into the pass. "Oh, look. She is sitting up. I should see if she is all right."

Fargo went along. He wouldn't mind an excuse to slug the bitch again.

Paloma had her elbows on her knees and her head was in her hands. She regarded Fargo as a rattlesnake might regard prey. "You hurt me, senor."

"Not bad enough," Fargo said.

"I will never forgive you. Not for hitting me, not for letting the Mother Superior die, not for my sister."

"What I have done does not concern you," Dalila said.

"On the contrary. You have shamed our family. Mother has told everyone that you were going off to join the convent. Now everyone will wonder, and people will talk, and before long everyone will know you are a slut."

Dalila balled her fists. "Watch that tongue of yours, *hermana*."

Paloma sneered at her. "If I am not afraid of the banditos and I am not afraid of the big oaf next to you, do you honestly think I would be afraid of you? You are upset because the truth hurts."

"Making love to a man does not make a woman a whore."

"Not in your eyes, perhaps. But in my eyes there are only two kinds of women in this world. Saints like the Mother Superior and sinful cows like our mother."

"You are sick," Dalila said.

Paloma proudly raised her head. "I am the one who is still a virgin."

"All these years, I never suspected how twisted you are. You're the opposite of the Mother Superior. She loved everyone. You hate everyone. She was kind. You are cruel. You no more deserve to wear a habit than I do."

"You're just jealous because I am a better person than you. I have stayed pure where you have not."

Fargo had had enough of Paloma's bile. He poured the last of the coffee into his cup, returned to the flat boulder, and marked time as the bandits doggedly climbed. The sun was at its zenith when they emerged from the last belt of timber and drew rein. He made no attempt to hide. Bartolo pointed, and all their faces swung toward him. Setting down the cup, he stood and moved to the opening in the notch.

Fargo raised the Henry.

Dying time was here.

18

The banditos dismounted and spread out. Bristling with weapons, they advanced until they were almost in rifle range. At a bellow from Fermin Terreros, they halted. Then, to Fargo's considerable surprise, Terreros gave his rifle and revolver to Yago, held his arms out from his sides, and came on alone.

Fargo squatted. He suspected a trick but he couldn't figure how. They couldn't get behind him or come at him from either side. The only way was straight up and there was little cover. The few boulders weren't big enough to offer much concealment. He centered the sights on Terreros's chest and when Terreros was as near as he would allow, he shouted, "Close enough."

The bandit leader stopped. "Gringo," he said.

"What do you want?"

Terreros pushed his sombrero back. "You should have kept going. Now we can kill you without half trying."

"Might take more than half," Fargo said.

"I didn't come up here to waste words on you. I would like to speak to Angelina, *por favor.*"

"Maybe she doesn't want to speak to you," Fargo said.

The other bandits hadn't moved. Some were fingering their pistols and long guns.

"She would never refuse me," Terreros said smugly. "Not after what we once meant to each other."

Fargo could have told the truth, that the nun was dead. But something told him that if he did, he would regret it. So he bluffed. "Yell to her. She can hear you."

"I prefer face-to-face."

"Ever seen a Conestoga?" Fargo asked.

Terreros's eyebrows pinched together. "The big wagons with the canvas tops? What do they have to do with this?"

"I trust you about as far as I can throw one."

"So you will not permit me to come all the way up?" Terreros sighed. "Very well. In your position, I would probably do the same." He raised his voice. "Angelina! Hear me! I know what you think of me but I do not hold it against you. My fight is not with you. It is with this gringo. You can go on to the convent if you want. My men will not touch you. I, Fermin Rodriquez Terreros, give you his solemn word."

"What about the sisters?" Fargo said.

"The other nuns?"

"No. Dalila and Paloma."

"Oh. Them." Terreros made a dismissive gesture. "My men look forward to having fun with them."

"Then Sister Angelina stays here," Fargo said. "And if she's hit by a stray bullet, it will be your fault."

"It is for her to say whether she stays or goes," Terreros said. "Or would you hold her against her will?"

"I'll do whatever it takes."

"*Cabrón,*" Terreros hissed. "What manner of man are you that you would let a kind woman like her come to harm?"

"Pots and kettles," Fargo said.

"What the hell does that mean?" Terreros raised his voice again. "Angelina! Speak to me! If you want to go, this gringo won't stop you. My men and I will see to that."

"Go back down and start shooting," Fargo said. "When she's hit I'll let you know."

Terreros commenced to swear viciously in Spanish, then abruptly stopped and glanced to Fargo's right.

Fargo had a sinking feeling who he would see when he looked. "What the hell are you doing here?"

Paloma's arms were folded and she was looking down in disdain on Fermin Terreros. "Why do you keep shouting for the Mother Superior?"

"I want to talk to her, foolish one."

"You are the fool," Paloma said. "Or hasn't this stupid gringo told you that she has passed on?"

It was as if a lightning bolt cleaved Terreros. "What did you just say?"

"Mother Superior is dead. Her body is in the pass, covered with rocks by him." Paloma jerked a thumb at Fargo. "She had been ill for a great many months and didn't tell anyone."

"Dead?" Terreros said bleakly.

"*Sí*. Yet there you stand, yelling for her, when her ears cannot hear you." Paloma laughed. "I understand she thought highly of you once. It must have made you mad, her giving up a worthless drop of pig shit like you to serve our Lord."

The bandit leader took a half step back as if she had punched him. "You dare talk to me like that? To me? Fermin Terreros?"

"I will talk to you any way that suits me. Now that you have learned she is gone, ride off and leave us be."

"Ride off?" Terreros repeated, and turned red from his neck to his hairline. "*Ride off*? You pathetic little bitch. Before I am done with you, you will feel pain as no human being ever has." He looked at Fargo. "And you, gringo. *Que eres listo*. Very clever of you to make me think she was still alive. You played with my feelings for her, eh? In the hope I might let all of you go?"

Fargo said nothing.

Fermin Terreros did the last thing Fargo expected—he grinned. "It was a trick worthy of me. But it has failed, thanks to the bitch."

"Stop calling me that," Paloma said. "I'm going to be a nun like the Mother Superior."

"You—a Sister of Grace?" Terreros barked a cold chortle. "You are not fit to lick their shoes clean. I am doing them a favor." He turned to go and got off a last barb. "I did not think it was possible, girl, to want to kill anyone more than I want to kill the gringo, but now I want to kill you even more than him."

Fargo turned to Paloma and sighed. "If stupid was gold you'd be rich."

"I spoke the truth, didn't I? That's what a nun does."

"Who are you kidding?" Fargo said. "Terreros would make a better nun than you."

Paloma wheeled and stalked into the pass.

All hell would break loose now. Fargo stretched out on

his belly. He must make each shot tell. He saw Yago and Bartolo and some of the others come to meet Terreros. A heated exchange took place, ending when the bandits went to their horses and led the animals into the timber. Puzzling, that. Fargo thought for sure they would charge up the slope with their guns blazing.

For a while all was quiet. Then Fargo heard snapping and cracking noises, as of a lot of tree limbs being broken. Bandits reappeared, their arms full of firewood, which they heaped in large piles spaced about fifty feet apart.

Fargo guessed what they were up to. He had to hand it to Terreros. The bandit leader was clever as hell. The question was whether they would try before the sun went down, or after. His money was on after.

As the minutes crawled into an hour and an hour into two, Fargo knew he was right. The piles had grown to bonfire size. Every now and then Terreros would look up at the pass, and smile. Yago did a lot of looking, too, through his spyglass. Once, Fargo raised his hand and pretended to shoot a pistol. Yago raised his hand with a finger in the air.

Pebbles rattled, and Dalila crawled out next to him. "It's been so long. What are they waiting for?"

"Dark."

"What are all those piles for? So they'll have light to shoot?"

"So they'll have smoke," Fargo said. "Most of the woods is green pine."

"My offer to help was sincere. Anything I can do, I will."

"Have you beat your sister with a rock yet?"

"I would if she was still here."

Fargo was so intent on the bandits that for a few seconds he didn't realize what she had said. He turned with a start. "Paloma is gone?"

Dalila nodded. "I was napping and she woke me to say she wasn't going to stay and be killed. She went out the other end of the pass half an hour ago."

Fargo knew that on foot, in the Sangre de Cristos, Paloma wouldn't last long. Thirst and hunger would do her in, if the wild beasts or worse didn't get to her first. "Didn't you try to stop her?"

"No. I am tired of her treating me like the dirt under her feet. I did point out that she was the one who wanted us to stay and protect Mother Superior's body, and she said she only told you that so you would fight the bandits to the last and give her and me time to get away."

"She and Terreros are more alike than they'll admit," Fargo said.

"It is just the two of us now against all of those banditos with their guns and knives. It does not look good, does it?"

"We're still breathing," Fargo said, which was about as optimistic as he could be under the circumstances.

"Whatever happens, I thank you for, well, you know. I was right not to want to be a nun. I could not do without it my whole life long. How anyone can is a mystery to me."

"Makes two of us," Fargo said.

"If we live you can make love to me again if you like." Dalila chuckled. "I would not resist you, ever."

To the west, the sun dipped. A blunt snout of shadow crept from the pass toward the timber. The trees became dark well before the sun was gone. The bandits lit torches and Terreros positioned men next to each of the piles. Rifles and pistols were checked. Knives were honed.

"It is as if they prepare for war," Dalila said.

"I want you in the pass," Fargo said. "If they get past me, run."

"I would rather stay by your side."

"No." Fargo reached over and squeezed her arm. "I can't fight them and keep an eye on you. It would get me killed sooner."

"Very well." Dalila slid closer and kissed him on the cheek. "Be careful, my handsome lover. I have grown very fond of you."

"Just so you don't ask me to marry you."

Dalila laughed. For a few heartbeats the worry vanished from her face. Then she gazed down the mountain and frowned. "God in heaven. How did we get into this mess?"

"Your mother."

"I should have stood up for myself. I should have refused to go. From now on I will never do anything unless I truly want to do it." She swiveled and crawled off.

Fargo was racking his brain for anything that would help him. It was too bad Sister Angelina had died. She might have persuaded Terreros to— A tingle of inspiration ran down his spine. "Dalila," he said quickly.

She looked back. "*Sí*, handsome one?"

"Uncover her."

"Sorry?"

"Angelina. Take off all the rocks."

"What good will that do? Didn't my sister tell Fermin Terreros that the Mother Superior is dead?"

"Just do it."

"Very well. But it is loco, if you ask me."

All Fargo could do now was wait. There were four piles of wood. Enough to create a lot of cover. The wind had to be right, though, blowing from the bandits toward the pass and not the other way around. At the moment the wind was still.

The sun was almost gone. Twilight was settling. Terreros took to pacing with his hands behind his back. Waiting for the wind, Fargo reckoned. Darkness had blanketed the valley floor when he felt the breeze on his cheeks.

Terreros roared commands. Torches were applied to the piles. Crackling and sizzling, the branches caught. The flames grew rapidly. As they grew, the smoke spread. At first only puffs and then small clouds that bulged and spread and became large clouds that formed into a bank much like fog. Slowly, like a giant gray slug creeping on invisible tendrils and devouring the ground it covered, the smoke crawled toward the pass.

Fargo estimated it would take about ten minutes to reach him. He was tempted to plunge down into it and try to reach the woods, and the Ovaro. But he couldn't leave Dalila unprotected.

Terreros was shouting again. Telling his men to be ready. Telling them to stay low and to be careful not to shoot one another. "If you can take the gringo alive, so much the better," he yelled. "If not, that is fine, too."

The breeze had picked up. The smoke was moving faster.

"Do you hear me up there, gringo?" Terreros yelled. "We are coming for you. Your luck has run out."

Fargo cupped a hand to his mouth. "She wants me to tell you that she will never forgive you for this."

"Who?" Terreros hollered.

"Sister Angelina."

"What the hell are you talking about, gringo? She's dead. The *chica* told me. You were there."

"She lied."

Terreros blistered the air with oaths. "What game are you playing at, gringo? Are you trying to confuse me?"

"It was the girl's doing."

"Why would she make up such a thing?"

"She hates you, is why. She'd say anything to make you mad." Fargo congratulated himself. That was a good touch.

"If Angelina is truly alive, have her call down to me."

The smoke was forty feet out.

"Have her come out and say something, damn you."

Fargo cupped his hand again. "I don't want her where she can take a stray bullet. I'll relay whatever she wants."

"I am waiting!" Terreros shouted, almost eagerly.

Fargo let a minute go by, then yelled down, "Angelina says the girl was right. You *are* a worthless pile of pig shit."

An inarticulate roar of rage came out of the smoke. Then silence for the pause it took Fermin Terreros to catch his breath. "Now, *mi amigos*! Kill the gringo! I want his blood! I want his guts! I want him dead, dead, dead!"

19

Backlit by the inferno glow of the bonfires, the smoke seemed to pulse with orange and red light. In its depths dark figures advanced, slowly. The bandits weren't about to rush headlong into Fargo's gun sights, no matter what Terreros wanted.

Fargo fixed a bead on one of the shapes. He held his breath to steady his arms and smoothly squeezed the trigger. At the blast, the figure lurched as if rising onto the tips of its boots, and pitched over. Fargo was already in motion, rolling to the right in case the muzzle flash gave him away. It did. Rifles boomed and six-shooters cracked. He jacked the lever, fired again, then heaved up and backed into the notch. More lead sought him, whining off rocks. Hornets promised buzzing death close to his ears.

"He got Carlos!" someone shouted.

Fargo shot at the shouter. He sidestepped, fired, and dived flat. More slugs whistled over him.

Terreros shouted something, and suddenly the shooting stopped. The figures melted away, as if into the earth.

Fargo suspected that was exactly what they had done. The bandits had gone to ground and were on their bellies, crawling toward him. The smoke had helped them but it also hindered them; to kill him they would have to get close.

Fargo crabbed backward. The smoke flowed over him. Thick as gravy, it burned his eyes and throat. He stifled a cough that would give him away. Sliding his right leg behind him, he bumped something.

"Be careful," Dalila said. "You nearly kicked me in the head."

Fargo turned. He had to practically touch his face to hers to see her. "Time for you to leave."

"You said to flee if they get past you."

"They're almost on us. Go out the other end of the pass and wait for me." Fargo gave her a push.

"I am better off staying with you. I know you don't want me to but—" Dalila stopped and broke into a fit of uncontrollable coughing. She covered her mouth with her hand but the harm had been done.

Flashes of flame punctuated the smoke. Fargo replied with lead of his own. He reared onto his knees to shield Dalila and felt a tug at his sleeve. She grunted, and groaned. A slug had nicked him and struck her. Wrapping his arm around her waist, he retreated. He came to Sister Angelina's body, which Dalila had uncovered as he'd asked. He set Dalila down. "How bad are you hit?"

"My arm. It's not deep."

Movement in the smoke warned Fargo to hurry her along. "Go. Now. I'll catch up." He pushed her harder.

For once Dalila didn't argue. Holding her arm, blood trickling from between her fingers, she ran.

The smoke swirled and disgorged an apparition in a sombrero. Fargo and the bandit fired at the same instant. The bandit missed. Fargo didn't. He levered a round into the chamber but no more appeared. Hunkering, he got hold of the habit and began to drag the body toward the other end of the notch. A pistol banged but the shot didn't come close.

From the valley side rose another bellow from Terreros. "Why haven't you killed him yet? He is only one hombre."

"It is the smoke," someone answered.

"A thousand pesos out of my own pocket for the man who brings the gringo down!" Terreros spurred them on.

Fargo stepped on a rock that slid away from under him, and nearly fell. Stopping, he braced for shots that didn't ring out. He firmed his hold and he hurried on. The smoke thinned, and he could breathe again. He gratefully gulped air. He reached the end and looked for Dalila below, only to have her sprout next to him.

"Here I am, handsome one."

"You don't listen worth a damn."

"I refuse to desert you." Dalila still had her hand over the wound and was grimacing in pain.

"Suit yourself." Fargo shoved the Henry at her and when she took it, he stooped and placed the body so it appeared to be sitting up. He had to force the arms to move, they were so stiff. The same with the legs.

"What in God's name are you doing?"

"A decoy for the ducks," Fargo said. "There. That should do it." He grasped Dalila's wrist and headed down the slope to a cluster of boulders. Propping his elbows, he aligned the Henry's sights on the nun's back.

"You are a devil," Dalila said.

Fargo concentrated on the notch. A tongue of smoke ebbed over Sister Angelina and licked down the mountain. Stick shapes acquired substance, and a man called out excitedly.

"Jefe! It is her! Angelina!"

The shapes formed a half ring around the body. Through them shouldered another: Fermin Terreros.

"Out of my way, damn you. Let me see her."

Fargo could just make Terreros out. He saw him stop in shock, saw him bend and reach out to the corpse.

"Angelina? Why do you not speak?"

His finger to the trigger, Fargo centered the sights a few inches above the nun's head.

He still couldn't see Terreros clearly.

"She *is* dead!" the bandit leader roared, and straightened.

Fargo fired.

The impact jolted Terreros back into the smoke. Whether he fell or not, Fargo couldn't tell. He ducked as the other bandits let loose a firestorm. Ricochets pinged and screeched.

Twenty, thirty, forty shots, the fusillade followed by ear-ringing silence.

Fargo risked a peek over the boulder. The bandits were gone. "Stay here," he instructed Dalila. "And this time I mean it."

"Do not worry," she said through clenched teeth. "I hurt too much to go anywhere."

The nun's body was on its side. A stray slug had smashed the forehead and a fluid that made Fargo think of pus was oozing out. He stepped over it. The pass was solid smoke. Warily, he crept after the bandits, stopping when voices grated in anger.

"How bad are you hurt, jefe?"

That sounded like Yago.

"In the belly," Terreros rasped. "Take me out and find Slate. He has cut bullets out before."

"You heard him, Bartolo. Get moving."

Fargo mentally counted to twenty and glided after them. He breathed through his mouth in short shallow breaths. A cough helped him avoid a lagging shape. Then he was out of the pass and on the slope. The bonfires still crackled. Angling wide, he reached the timber.

Not much smoke was in the trees, and he spotted the horses right away.

Beyond, in a clearing, Yago and several others were lowering Terreros onto a blanket. Terreros tossed his head, and cursed.

"Easy, damn you! The pain is terrible."

Belly wounds were nearly always fatal. Sometimes the person lasted for days, suffering terrible torment. Fargo could have aimed higher. He hadn't.

"Madre de Dios!" Terreros cried out in agony.

Fargo neared the horses. No one appeared to be guarding them. The bandits were gathered around their stricken leader. He counted eight, one of them with an arm in a crude sling.

Slate knelt and drew a knife. He pried at Terreros's shirt and examined the hole and then looked up at the others and shook his head.

"Dig it out," Terreros commanded. His fingers clawed the earth and he hissed through his nose.

"It's no use, boss."

"I didn't ask you. I told you. Dig the goddamn bullet out."

"It's made a mess of your innards," Slate said. "Looks like it bounced off one of your conchos and tore you all to hell. I dig it out, I'll just make things worse."

Terreros stopped hissing and drew his revolver. He pointed it at Slate and cocked the hammer. "I will die for certain if we do nothing. Dig the goddamn lead out or you will die before me."

"Do it," Yago said.

Slate didn't look happy. "Some of you hold him down. I can't have him bucking while I dig."

Fargo reached the Ovaro. He patted the stallion's neck.

"God, I hurt," Terreros said.

The reins were wrapped around a sapling. Fargo unwound them and quietly slid the Henry into the saddle scabbard. He moved to a second horse, a bay, and took its reins in his other hand.

Four men had taken hold of Terreros's arms and legs. Slate inserted his knife into the wound and Terreros started to scream. Someone wedged a stick into his mouth and he bit down, stifling it.

Fargo thought of all the people the bandit leader had killed. He thought of all the misery and suffering Terreros had inflicted. And he smiled as he led the horses away.

He didn't make straight for the pass. He went north through the timber until it was safe for him to climb on and then he circled to come at the pass from the side.

By now the bonfires were low, the smoke reduced to writhing serpents. A body with part of its face blown away lay near the notch. Another was sprawled stomach down with a hole in the back of its head.

Fargo didn't look at the nun as he went past. He descended to the boulders quickly and was puzzled when Dalila didn't step out. He called her name.

There was no reply.

"Dalila? Let's get the hell out of here." Dismounting, Fargo searched, but she was gone. He looked up the mountain. He looked down the mountain. "What the hell?"

Fargo opened his saddlebags so he could take out ammunition for the Henry. His fingers brushed something that hadn't been there before. He took it out and held it in his palm, and grinned in delight. "I'll be damned." It was his Colt. He put Yago's revolver in the saddlebag, verified his own was loaded, and twirled it into his holster. He reloaded the Henry, slid it back into the scabbard, and climbed on the Ovaro. He felt whole again.

"Dalila?" Fargo tried once more. He doubted she had traipsed off on her own. He wondered if maybe Paloma had come back and the two of them had gone off together. He rode down the mountain, taking it slow, the reins to the bay in his left hand. Vegetation sprouted in the form of scrub brush and stunted trees.

After only a hundred yards, Fargo stopped. It was pointless to blunder around in the dark.

An open space in a patch of brush was as likely a spot as any. He dismounted and hunkered with the Henry across his legs. Over an hour went by and the only sounds were the distant keen of coyotes and once the bleat of a deer.

Fargo was growing concerned. But there was nothing he could do. Blundering around in the dark was pointless. He eased onto his back with an arm under his head. He would get a little rest. No sooner did he close his eyes than he was sucked into a black emptiness that lasted until the caw of a raven woke him at the crack of the new day. His body felt sluggish and his mind was mush. He dearly needed coffee. Instead, he climbed on the Ovaro and returned to the boulders where he had last seen Dalila. The ground was hard and rocky and he had about decided he was wasting his time when he came on a clear print in the dust.

"Hell."

The shape of the moccasin left no doubt. An Apache had her. The toes pointed down the mountain.

Hoping against hope, Fargo rode hard. Now and then he came on another track, or a partial. They were too obvious. No Apache would leave so much sign unless he wanted it to be seen.

When Fargo first noticed a large oak in the distance he didn't think much of it. Oaks were everywhere. But when he saw that the tracks led in the oak's direction, he rose in the stirrups and made out a splash of yellow under the limbs.

Fargo stopped. She was being used as bait, much as he had used the nun's body.

He shucked the Henry and proceeded at a walk until he was close enough to see that Dalila was tied to the tree, her head down, either passed out or dead. Strips had been cut from her dress to tie her, and her hair was a tangled mess.

Fargo drew rein and swung down. The ground around the oak was bare except for a few small bushes. It seemed there was nowhere to hide but Fargo knew better. Apaches were masters at concealing themselves where it didn't seem possible. He peered into the branches. He sidled to the right and checked behind the trunk. He examined the bushes. Nothing. Nothing at all.

"Dalila?"

She hung limp, her hair over her face.

Fargo held the Henry in his left hand, the stock against his thigh to brace it, and drew his Colt.

"Dalila? Answer me if you can."

Her dress was torn at the shoulder and she had bruises on her shoulder and on the left side of her face.

Fargo took a step and stopped. He took another step and did the same. When it happened it would happen fast. He kept glancing to either side and over his shoulder and at the oak and past it. He was a mouse being lured by cheese. He hated it but it had to be done. His nerves were as taut as wire. He made it halfway. Scarlet drops on the lemon yellow of her dress brought a rush of new worry. It could be her throat was slit but he couldn't tell for all the hair.

"Dalila?"

Fargo took several steps at once. He knew he shouldn't. He glanced right but he didn't glance left. The next instant the earth to his left erupted. A shade slow in reacting, Fargo whirled.

The warrior had used a trick, one among many, that the Apaches were masters at—he had dug down deep enough for him to lie on his back, then covered himself with dirt. From an early age Apaches were taught how to do it so that they appeared to be part of the ground around them.

Now, with a piercing cry and a knife raised to stab, the Apache attacked with all the ferocity of his warrior breed.

20

Fargo swept the Henry's barrel up to deflect the blow. Metal rang on metal. The force rocked him; the warrior was immensely strong. Fargo dodged a stab at his throat and retreated to gain room to level the Henry but the Apache came after him. The knife sliced at his middle. This time he warded the blade off with the Henry's stock. The blade glanced off and he felt a sharp sting in his leg. He had been cut. It threw him off-balance and he stumbled.

The Apache lowered a shoulder and rammed into him.

Down Fargo went, crashing onto his back with the warrior on top. He drove the Henry at the Apache's jaw but it had no effect. The warrior's other hand found his throat and locked fast. Iron fingers dug into his windpipe, blocking off his breath. He heaved but the Apache was too heavy. The knife arced at his neck. He got his arm up and gripped a thick wrist. Both of them strained.

"Dee-dah tatsan," the warrior hissed.

Fargo knew some Apache. "You die now," the warrior had said. And he would, too, unless . . .

The warrior threw all his weight into bearing down with the blade.

Fargo slammed his forehead into the warrior's face, once at the nose and again at the mouth. Wet drops fell. The Apache grunted and his knife arm weakened. Fargo punched him in the throat. The warrior reared back. Fargo grabbed the knife arm, twisted, and rolled. Now they were side to side on their shoulders, the warrior red in the face and gasping for breath. Fargo jabbed a finger into an eye and the Apache jerked his head back. Quickly, Fargo tucked his right leg to his chest and his hand found his ankle sheath. The Apache's blade missed his throat. Lunging, Fargo buried the toothpick to the hilt under the warrior's chin and blood gushed hot and red.

The Apache scrambled away and made it to his hands and knees. He looked at Fargo as if puzzled by the outcome, and pitched over.

Fargo rose. He switched the toothpick to his left hand and drew the Colt. He had worried there were more warriors than one but apparently there weren't.

The Apache was weakly wheezing. Crimson mist sprayed from the hole with each breath. He reached up as if trying to touch the sky, and died.

Fargo wiped the toothpick on the warrior's breechclout. Retrieving the Henry, he hurried to the tree. "Dalila?" Her head still hung low. He leaned the Henry against the oak and holstered the Colt and felt for a pulse. There was one, strong and steady. He ran his hand over her head. Behind her left ear was a large knot. It explained why she was unconscious. Cutting her free, he eased her to the ground. She moaned but didn't move when he shook her.

Fargo fetched the waterskin. He untied his bandanna, wet it, and applied it to her face. She was a while reviving. When she came around she blinked and looked down at herself.

"Where am I? What happened?"

"An Apache," Fargo said.

Fear filled Dalila's eyes. "Now I remember!" She started to raise her head. "Where is he?"

"Dead," Fargo said, and nodded at the body.

Dalila sank back. "You came after me."

"He made it easy," Fargo said. "He wanted my guns and my horse."

Frowning, she touched the goose egg. "He came out of nowhere and hit me so hard, I thought I had died."

"Was he alone?" Fargo asked the crucial question.

"I didn't see any others."

Fargo held the waterskin so she could drink. She had been lucky. So had he.

If there had been more than one, the outcome would have been different. When she had enough he hung the waterskin on his saddle. "As soon as you're able, we're lighting a shuck."

"My sister?" Dalila asked.

"No sign of her."

"Where can she have gotten to?"

Fargo gazed out over the vast expanse of the Sangre de Cristos. "Anywhere." He didn't rate Paloma's prospects very high.

"The banditos?"

"They won't let us reach Santa Fe if they can help it."

"So we are not out of danger yet?"

Fargo was honest with her. "Far from it."

"Mother Superior, dead. My own sister, missing. All because my mother got it into her head that her daughters should be holy." Tears seeped from the corners of Dalila's eyes. "Never again will I let anyone tell me how I should live my life."

Fargo sympathized. He had an independent streak in him as wide as the Mississippi. He refused to live by anyone's notion but his own.

"You've gone through a lot on our behalf. I am sorry for all the trouble it has caused you."

"You have five minutes to rest," Fargo said. He rose and walked in a circle around the large oak. In three directions the emptiness was undisturbed. To the east men and horses shimmered in the glare of the sun.

Dalila was sitting up when he came around the tree. "My head is pounding but I'm fit enough to ride."

"Good girl." Fargo held off telling her about the four riders until she was on the bay and they were under way.

Dalila turned in the saddle. "Bandits, no?"

"Bandits, yes."

"Will they catch us?"

"We're days from Santa Fe."

"So they will. And all we can do is pick the spot to make our stand."

"You're learning," Fargo said.

It was noon when they stopped to rest. The shimmering figures were bigger. A bright gleam told Fargo that Yago was using the spyglass. He drank sparingly but let Dalila have as much as she wanted.

Fargo was surprised that as the afternoon waxed, the ban-

149

dits didn't gain. The sun was a hand's-width above the horizon when it hit him why: they were holding back, staying out of rifle range, waiting for dark.

Dalila's chin kept dropping and she would snap her head up to keep from falling asleep.

"I don't know how much longer I can hold out."

"Do the best you can."

"Find a spot soon," she urged.

A mountain lion picked it for them. Fargo happened to glance up and there the big cat was, staring down from a high ledge. He reined toward it and the cougar ran off. The climb was treacherous but worth it. He had a clear line of fire, and to get around behind them the bandits would have to ride around the mountain.

Dalila had more water and applied his wet bandanna to her brow and her neck.

"How long before this awful headache goes away?"

"When it's good and ready."

Stretching out, Fargo folded his arms and rested his chin on them. It would be half an hour yet.

"Are those vultures?"

Fargo squinted at dark V's circling with outspread wings. "Looks to be," he said.

"Do you think they know? That they can sense blood is going to be spilled and people are going to die?"

"They have brains the size of a pea."

"I'm sorry. I'm scared, and when I'm scared, I talk a lot." Dalila laid down next to him. "I wish I was home. I wish it more than anything. I never realized how good my life was. But now, after poor Mother Superior, my sister missing, and those banditos and that Apache . . ." She stopped and put her face in her hands and wept.

Fargo let her cry. She'd been through hell and it would do her good. He watched the approaching riders. When they were still a ways off he recognized three of the four: Yago, Bartolo and Slate. The fourth man wore a sombrero and had a bandolier across his chest and what appeared to be a Sharps rifle. That was worrisome. A Sharps could shoot farther than the Henry. He'd owned one once. Sharps were remarkably accurate in the hands of someone who knew how to use them. He suspected that the bandit knew how.

Dalila stopped crying and lay quiet. After a while she rose on her elbows and mopped at her face. "They're almost here."

"When I tell you, take the horses as far back as you can go," Fargo instructed her.

The ledge was about twenty-five feet wide at the broadest point. She and the animals would be safe so long as he kept the bandits from climbing too high.

"Once again you are about to risk your life for me."

"My hide's at stake too." Fargo raised the Henry and held it so the sun sparkled on the brass receiver.

"You did that to remind them you have a rifle," Dalila said. "So they won't come too close."

"Maybe you should be a scout."

Dalila laughed, then asked, "How can you be so calm?"

Fargo shrugged. "You live in the wild, you get used to this."

"To what? To the killing? To the blood and the violence?" Dalila shook her head. "I never could. I don't see how you do."

The bandits drew rein about five hundred yards away. They dismounted and Yago smiled up and waved. The rest tended to their weapons.

"Take the horses and move back," Fargo said.

"Be careful. If anything should happen to you . . ." Dalila didn't finish. She lightly touched him, then grabbed both reins.

Yago was unbuckling his gun belt. He handed it to Bartolo and Bartolo gave him a rifle with a brown bandanna tied at the end of the barrel. Holding the rifle aloft and moving it back and forth, Yago came up the mountain as if out for a Sunday stroll. He had his hat pushed back so his curly hair spilled from under it, and he showed more teeth than a politician courting votes.

When he was within earshot he shouted merrily, "Gringo! I have a few things to say."

He climbed until he was ten feet below the ledge. "See? I come under a flag of truce."

"The flag is supposed to be white."

"The only white we had was an old sock of Slate's and I

was not about to touch the filthy thing." Yago worked the lever on the rifle to show it was empty. "My weapon is empty. You need have no fear this is a trick."

"My weapon isn't. I could shoot you."

"But you won't."

"What makes you so sure?"

"Because you are curious about why I have been so bold. And you are like me, I think, in that you do not shoot men who cannot shoot back."

"A noble bandit."

Yago laughed. "I am many things, gringo, but noble is not one of them." He leaned on the rifle and took an exaggerated deep breath. "It is a glorious day, no?"

"You're in a good mood."

"Why should I not be?" Yago said. "Thanks to you, senor, I am now the leader of what the gringo sheriff liked to call the Terreros gang. Now it is the Yago gang. My gang. And do you know what? I find I like being in charge. I like telling the others what to do."

"Not many of them left," Fargo said.

"Enough. But the others would not come with us. They think you are bad medicine, as the Indians say."

"So there's just the four of you?"

Yago grinned. "Forget about them. I have news you will like."

"Try me," Fargo said.

"Terreros died a bad death. We tried to cut the bullet out but it had gone through his belly and was stuck in his spine." Yago didn't sound sad about it. "Fermin was not very brave at the end. He screamed and cursed you and then he cried like a *bebé*. Like a baby. That was when I shot him in the head."

"To put him out of his misery."

"He embarrassed us, to weep like that."

"Congratulations on the promotion."

"*Gracias*, senor. And now that I am in charge, things are different. I do not hate you as Fermin did. The nun meant nothing to me."

"What about the bruises on your face?"

Yago touched them. "So you hit me? Men like us, fighting

is what we do. I do not hold a grudge. To prove it, I will let you live."

"Saint Yago," Fargo said.

"I am being practical. We try to kill you, more of us might die, and we have already lost too many. You are tricky, senor. And very deadly."

Fargo waited.

Yago rose onto his toes to try and see more of the ledge. "One of the girls is with you, yes? The pretty one. I saw her through my telescope." He paused. "What happened to the other *chica*?"

"She strayed off."

"She was dumb, that one. But no matter. It is the pretty one we want." Yago beamed. "Hand her over to us and you can be on your way."

"Just like that?" Fargo said, and snapped his fingers.

"*Sí.* Just like that." Yago snapped his. "After all the trouble we have had, we are due that much, at least. Besides, what is she to you? It was the nun who hired you, yes? Give us the girl and we will ride off and you will never see us again."

"No."

"As a token, senor." Yago glanced down at the other bandits. "To show them that you have respect for me."

"You're a gob of spit," Fargo said.

Yago lost his smile. He scowled, and his knuckles on the rifle were white. "Now see? I tried to make peace with you. I offered you your life and you threw it in my face."

"What are you really up to?"

Yago sighed. "You would make a good bandito, as suspicious as you are." He shouldered the rifle. "But I am wasting my time. Very well. You want to die for the girl, that is your affair." He wheeled and started down. "You have made your choice and now you must live with it. Or die with it maybe, eh?" And Yago laughed.

21

The bandits made no attempt to rush the ledge. They didn't fire a shot. They sat near their horses and talked.

Fargo didn't like it. They were up to something. They might be waiting for the sun to set as they had done at the pass but he couldn't see the four of them charging up the open slope even in the dark. He rolled onto his back and studied the mountain above the ledge. It reared another thousand feet, barren and stark and virtually sheer. Getting up it, on this side, was next to impossible.

Dalila crawled over. "What is the matter? You look worried."

"They're not doing anything."

"They're scared of you. They don't want to die just to get their hands on me. Maybe they'll ride off and in a couple of days I'll be home."

"Could be," Fargo said without conviction. As soon as the sun went down he would cut up blankets to muffle the hooves of their horses and try to sneak away.

Another quarter of an hour had gone by when Yago stood and unfolded his telescope and trained it up the slope. He took a few steps and hollered, "Gringo! Are you awake up there?"

Fargo centered the Henry even though Yago was out of range. "I hear you."

"I gave you your chance and you didn't take it. Now I am afraid that as the new jefe I must make an example of you. To earn respect, yes? Stand up with your hands in the air. You and the girl, both."

"Is he loco?" Dalila said.

"I am waiting, gringo," Yago shouted.

"Go to hell."

"One day, perhaps. But there is something you should know. I lied about my other men. They did not stay behind. Can you guess where they are?"

Fargo glanced up the mountain. High on the rim sombreros were silhouetted against the sky. Rifles stuck over the side, pointed down.

"They're above us!" Dalila exclaimed.

"Get on your horse." Fargo ran to the Ovaro, shoved the Henry into the scabbard, and was mounted when the first boom from above heralded the smack of a heavy slug into the ledge.

Dalila had grabbed at the bay's reins but it shied. She tried again, and a second shot sent it trotting off in a panic.

Bending, Fargo offered his arm. "Quick. Swing up."

Dalila grabbed his wrist.

More rifles boomed. Small puffs of dust peppered the ledge.

Fargo spurred over the rim and down the slope at an angle that would take them clear of the bandits below. Those on the rim fired furiously, trying to drop the Ovaro. The lead sounded like hail.

Yago yelled and pointed and he and the other three ran for their animals.

Loose rocks and dirt cascaded from under the Ovaro's flying hooves. Dalila had her arms tight around Fargo's waist and was breathing in short frightened gasps.

The men up on the rim had stood and were shooting as fast as they could work their weapons.

The four bandits below were racing to cut them off.

Fargo's only hope was to get around the mountain and out of range. More shots cracked, from above and below.

"I am hit!" Dalila cried.

"We can't stop," Fargo said over his shoulder. Her eyes were wide with the shock and the pain. "Hold on."

"*Sí.*"

Boulders sprouted like giant eggs and blunt tombstones. Fargo galloped in among them and the firing faded. He nearly collided with a huge slab. "How are you holding up?" he shouted.

"I am fine," Dalila said, but she didn't sound fine. She said it in his ear so weakly, he barely heard her.

The bandits were hard after them. Fargo could hear them yelling and the rumble of artificial thunder. He burst out of the boulders onto a flat stretch and gave the Ovaro its head. By the time Yago and the other three appeared, he was far enough away that they didn't bother to shoot. They stopped, apparently to wait for their friends from the rim.

A mile of hard riding brought Fargo to woodland. Cottonwoods drew him to a ribbon of water with high banks. He drew rein on a gravel bar. While the stallion drank, he carried Dalila to a patch of grass and set her down.

"Let me have a look."

The slug had caught her high on the left shoulder. It had glanced off the clavicle and ruptured out her upper arm, taking a good-sized chunk of flesh. Fargo's first job was to stop the bleeding. He cut a strip from her dress, washed it in the stream, and applied it to stanch the flow.

"It never ends," Dalilia said.

"I'll get you out of this," Fargo promised. That there was only one way to be sure she was safe. That his own life might be forfeit, he kept to himself.

Separate bandages were required for the entry and exit holes. He also rigged a sling. When he was done he washed his hands.

Dalila had passed out.

Fargo covered her with his blanket. He had done all he could. Barring infection, or capture by the bandits, she should survive. He couldn't do anything about the first but he could about the second. He yanked the Henry out and walked back the way they had come.

The bandits, all eight, were taking their sweet time. Instead of spreading out, they were in a cluster except for a man in a sombrero who was out ahead, doing the tracking. Not that it was difficult with the tracks so fresh.

Fargo stepped into the open and stood side-on with the Henry raised. The man in the lead spotted him and yelled to the rest. Yago resorted to his spyglass. Fargo crooked a finger and beckoned.

The eight stopped.

Good shooters were accurate with a Henry out to a hundred yards. Exceptional shooters were accurate out to a hundred and fifty, or more. Fargo was better than good. He had won several matches to prove it. He tested the wind by licking his finger, and was ready.

The bandits broke into a long line. At a yell from Yago they came on at a walk until they were three hundred yards out. Yago shouted again and they brought their animals to a trot. At two hundred yards, and another bark from Yago, they charged at a gallop.

The bandit with the Sharps was Fargo's first target. The bandit fired but the rolling gait of his animal threw his aim off. Fargo, standing rock steady, put his slug where he wanted: in the man's head above the eyebrows.

Slate was Fargo's second target. Slate's rifle looked to be a Morse with a longer than common barrel, and longer usually equated to greater range. The Morse, and Slate, tumbled, flying over his animal's rump.

Now there were six. They fired like madmen. Fargo was forced into the trees. He jacked the Henry's lever and braced the barrel against a tree. Some of the bandits broke to the right, others to the left. Only one came straight on: Bartolo.

Fargo fired twice. His first seemed to have no effect. His second send blood spurting from Bartolo's neck and Bartolo flying from his saddle.

Five left, and they were almost to cover. Fargo had hoped to drop more. He got off a last shot but must have missed. Then the bandits were in the woods and the drum of hooves ceased.

They would come after him on foot. It was cat and mouse, and he was the mouse.

Crouching, Fargo worked to the left, moving from cover to cover. A brown sombrero broke the green of the vegetation. He filled the Henry's sights with the swarthy face under the hat, and fired.

Two rifles rapidly returned lead.

Fargo dived flat and snapped off a shot at a muzzle flash. He rolled and waited for another flash but the men had stopped. Crawling to a tree, he rose.

From the right came a crackle of brush. Yago and the last bandit were hurrying to help their friends.

Fargo was between them. He took off his hat and set it down. He leaned the Henry against the trunk. Carefully, he leaped up, caught hold of a low limb, and pulled himself high enough to see over most of the tangle. He spotted a man to the left, stalking in his direction.

Letting go, he reclaimed the Henry, sank to a knee, and sighted on where the man would appear.

In a few seconds a bulk was framed by spindly brush. He shot into the center of the bulk, heard a grunt, shot again, and the bulk fell and thrashed. The thrashing didn't last long.

Now there were three.

Fargo put on his hat and moved obliquely to the right. His whole body was like a coiled spring. The faintest sound, the slightest movement, brought him to a stop. Once it was a startled jay. He focused on the thicket the jay flew from but no one appeared.

After that silence reigned. Fargo reckoned the bandits had gone to ground and were waiting for him to blunder into their sights. He stayed where he was. When it came to patience he was second to none, not even Apaches.

Off to the left was a log. He had glanced at it several times, and the next time he did, it had acquired a bump in the middle. The bump had dark hair. He brought the Henry to bear on a bearded face with a thick nose. The bandit looked around and rose higher.

Fargo shot him in the nose. He immediately changed position. Flattening, he crawled under a small pine. He almost didn't fit but it was excellent cover. A bandit would have to be right on top of him to see him.

Another came slinking among the trees. Nervous, he moved in spurts and jerks. He held two pistols. He came close to the small pine and stopped. His dark eyes darting, he whispered to himself, "Where can the gringo be?"

"Peekaboo," Fargo said.

The bandit whirled.

Fargo shot him in the chest. The slug penetrated below the sternum and ripped through the chest like a hot knife through butter. The man staggered and blood exploded from his nostrils and from his mouth. He sought to aim his pistols but he collapsed, broke into spasms, and was still.

From the left another bandit charged, working a rifle. He had seen, and he knew Fargo was under the pine.

Fargo rolled out from under it. He aimed, planted lead, heaved to a knee even as his sleeve was seared. He fired twice and the bandit dived headfirst into the ground. The legs twitched just once.

Fargo wheeled to the right. Now only Yago was left. He went a few steps, and froze.

Boots pounded, receding rapidly. He gave chase. The pounding boots were replaced by pounding hooves. When he hurtled out of the woods the horse was already fifty yards away, Yago low over the saddle. Fargo snapped the Henry to his shoulder only to see Yago slip over the side. Part of an arm and a leg showed, that was all. He aimed at the arm and Yago slipped lower so that only his hand was on the saddle horn. The man could ride.

Fargo fired and the top of the horn slivered. The horse veered, mane and tail flying.

Fargo centered the sights on its neck but he didn't shoot.

Yago stayed low until he was out of range. Then he swung up and drew rein. His shout was faint. "All of them but me?"

Fargo lowered the Henry. "All of them but you."

Yago's teeth were white in the sun. "Damn you, gringo. I hope to God I never set eyes on you again."

"It's a big country," Fargo said.

"*Sí.* And if I ever hear you are in this part of it, I will dig a hole and crawl in and stay until I hear you have left." Yago laughed and waved and used the big rowels on his spurs to raise dust.

"*Vaya con diablo,*" Fargo said.

Dalila was still unconscious, her forehead hot to the touch. She had a high fever, which suggested that infection had set in. She needed a sawbones and medicine or she could very well die.

Fargo went in search of horses. The bandits had left several tied to trees. He gathered them and led them back and rigged a lead rope for the three and the Ovaro. Then, holding Dalila, he climbed on a sorrel, gripped the rope, and was on his way. When one horse tired he switched to another, and when he switched, he left the exhausted horse behind. He saved the Ovaro for last. By then he was but hours from Santa Fe. He reached it as dawn was breaking and was directed to a doctor's. The physician who answered his knocks had him carry Dalila into a cool room with a long table. The doctor asked a few questions and then shooed him out.

A nurse went for the mother.

Delores arrived just as the doctor emerged, wiping his hands on a cloth. She ignored Fargo and asked about her daughter. The doctor said he had cleaned the wound and stitched it, and that although there was a fever, the wound wasn't infected. He expected her to live.

Only then did Delores turn to Fargo. Hate danced in her gaze. "Where is the Mother Superior?"

"Dead."

"And my other sweet one, Paloma?"

"Maybe dead too."

"Maybe?"

"She went off on her own. Could be that the Apaches got hold of her."

"God," Delores said. "At least I still have Dalila. When she recovers I will find someone else to take her to the convent."

"She doesn't want to be a nun."

Delores colored. "Of course she does, you stupid gringo. I am her mother. I know what is best."

"You're a bitch," Fargo said.

Delores balled her fists and took a ponderous step. "Be careful how you speak to me. I don't care if you are a man."

"You don't care about anything or anyone except you."

"Bastard. Miserable stinking bastard."

Fargo yawned and arched his back. He was tired to his marrow. "The Sisters of Grace won't take Dalila now."

"Why not?" Delores smugly demanded.

"She's not a virgin anymore."

"What?"

"I fucked her."

Fargo smiled and nodded at the doctor and walked out. He breathed deep, then climbed on the Ovaro and made down the street toward a cantina he was fond of.

God, he needed a drink.

LOOKING FORWARD!
The following is the opening
section of the next novel in the exciting
Trailsman **series from Signet:**

THE TRAILSMAN #350
HIGH COUNTRY HORROR

---

*1863, Arizona Territory—where death comes in the dark
of night, and worse in the bright light of day.*

Skye Fargo was snapped out of a sound sleep by a whinny from the Ovaro.

He rose onto his elbows and gazed about his camp. The fire had nearly gone out; only a few embers glowed red. Overhead, a legion of stars sparkled like gems.

Inky shadows shrouded the surrounding woods. He glanced at the Ovaro.

"What did you do that for?"

The stallion seldom whinnied without cause. Fargo went on looking and listening and when nothing happened he rolled onto his side and pulled his blanket up.

They were high on the Mogollon Plateau in wild country, and it was early autumn. At that time of year the night air was chill.

No sooner did Fargo close his eyes than a far-off drumming caused him to open them again. He sat up, put his hat on, and rose. A big man, broad of shoulder and narrow of waist, he wore buckskins and boots and had a red bandanna around his neck. Bending, Fargo plucked his gun belt from the ground and strapped it on.

The drumming grew louder. Fargo stepped away from the embers to the edge of the trees so he was in darkness and put his hand on his Colt. It paid to be cautious where night riders were concerned. He reckoned there must be half a dozen or more and he was proven right when eight riders came along the rutted dirt track that was called a road in these parts, and drew rein at the clearing's edge.

"Lookee here," a man declared.

"A horse," another said.

They reined into the clearing. One man dismounted and stepped to where Fargo's saddle and blankets lay. "Someone was sleeping here but they're gone."

"No," Fargo said. "They're not." He showed himself, demanding, "Who are you and what do you want?"

The man who had dismounted swooped his hand to his revolver but before he could clear leather Fargo slicked the Colt and trained it on him. They all heard the click of the hammer.

"Try to jerk that six-shooter and you're dead," Fargo warned.

"Hold on, Harvey," said one of those on horseback. "Let's not provoke him. We could be mistaken."

"Take your hand off that six-shooter," Fargo said.

The man called Harvey scowled but complied.

Fargo kept his Colt on the would-be quick-draw artist and came closer. He had thought maybe they were cowboys but several wore suits and bowlers or derbies and others wore store-bought shirts and britches or homespun.

Townsmen and farmers, he reckoned. "What the hell is this about?"

"As if you don't know," said Harvey.

"I wouldn't rile me more than you have," Fargo told him.

Harvey was almost as tall as Fargo and a lot thicker through the middle. He wore a bowler atop curly hair that framed a square block of a face with a nose as big as a cucumber. His suit included a vest from which a gold watch chain dangled. "I don't like some saddle tramp telling me what to do."

"Harvey, please," said the rider who had spoken before. "Let me handle this, will you?"

"Sure, Tom," Harvey said. "Kiss his ass, why don't you?"

The rider kneed his horse a little closer. "I'm sorry, mister, to barge in on you like this but it's a matter of life and death. My name is Tom Wilson. We're all of us from Haven."

Fargo recollected a town by that name. Several had sprung up in the past few years in the deep valleys that penetrated the Mogollon Plateau. "What are you doing here?"

"We're hunting for a missing girl," Wilson said. "A young woman, actually. She's nineteen years old. Her name is Myrtle Spencer and she was wearing a blue dress when she was seen last."

"What do you mean, missing?"

The man called Harvey growled, "As if you don't know, you son of a bitch. Where is she?"

"Harvey," Wilson said. "You're not helping matters."

"I don't care." Harvey gestured angrily at Fargo. "I say we make him tell us what he did with her. And if he won't tell, then we string him up."

"I don't know any Myrtle Spencer," Fargo said.

Two other riders were edging their hands toward holsters. They were trying to be sneaky about it but they were as obvious as a charging buffalo.

Fargo took another step and extended the Colt so the muzzle gouged Harvey's brow. "I won't say this again. Tell your friends to sit real still while we sort this out or I will by-God splatter your brains."

Harvey stiffened. He glared at Fargo, then said, "You heard him, boys. Don't try anything. We'll hear what the bastard has to say."

Wilson turned to the other two. "Dugan. McNee. You're not helping matters. Let me do the talking and you behave yourselves." He smiled at Fargo. "My apologies, mister. But we're high-strung over that missing girl. She's as sweet as can be and we would hate for anything to happen to her."

"I don't know any Myrtle Spencer," Fargo repeated himself.

"That may be. But you wouldn't have to know her to abduct her," Wilson said.

"Do you see a woman around here anywhere?" Fargo asked in mild exasperation. "Use your damn heads."

"That's what I'm trying to do," Wilson said. "Would you mind terribly much if me and a few of the rest were to look around?"

"Suit yourselves," Fargo said. "But keep your hands away from your hardware." He nodded at Dugan and McNee. "All of you can look except those two and this one." He tapped the Colt against Harvey's forehead. "I want them where I can keep an eye on them."

"Hell," Harvey said.

"You brought it on yourself, Harve," Wilson said. He climbed down and commenced walking about the clearing. Two others, at his urging, went into the trees. They were back in a couple of minutes, shaking their heads. One of them said, "Not a sign of her."

Wilson turned to Fargo. "Would you care to explain who you are and what you're doing here?"

"That's none of your business." Fargo didn't poke his nose into the affairs of others and he would be damned if he would let anyone poke their nose into his.

"Please," Wilson said. "It's important. If you've done nothing wrong you have no reason to worry."

Fargo was trying to be reasonable. He resented Harvey but there *was* a woman missing, or so they claimed. "Don't you have a lawman in Haven?"

"Yes, we do, in fact. Marshal Tibbit. He is out with another search party. They went north and we came south." Wilson turned to the others. "I have an idea. Why don't one of you fetch the marshal while we keep an eye on this gentleman? Lawrence, would you mind?"

"No," a townsman said. "I'll be back as quick as I can." Reining around, he jabbed his heels against his animal and trotted up the road.

"Now then," Wilson said. "Why don't the rest of us make ourselves comfortable until Marshal Tibbit gets here? Is that all right by you, mister?"

Fargo reluctantly nodded. Lowering the Colt, he stepped back and twirled it into his holster. "I have coffee left if anyone wants some."

Wilson smiled and nodded. "That would be nice, yes. I'm not used to being up this late. It must be pushing midnight."

Fargo hunkered to rekindle the fire. He kept an eye on Harvey, who had gone over to Dugan and McNee; the three were huddled together, whispering. When the flames were crackling, he turned to Tom Wilson. "You say this woman went missing?"

"She lives in Haven with her mother and father. Works at the dry goods store. They say she went out to hush the dog, which was making a ruckus, and never came back in. When her parents went out they found the dog with its throat slit and poor Myrtle was nowhere to be seen."

"It was a big dog, too," a townsman mentioned. "Whoever killed it had to be awful quick or awful strong or both."

"It wasn't me," Fargo said.

"I don't think it was you, either," Wilson said, "but we'll let the marshal decide what to do with you."

"Could it have been hostiles?" Fargo asked. He was thinking of the Apaches. They had no love for the white man, or white woman.

"If it was, it's the first lick of trouble in a coon's age. We're a fair-sized town and the heathens leave us be."

Harvey, Dugan and McNee came up and the former snapped at Wilson, "Why are you being so friendly? For all we know, he took Myrtle and she's lying out there somewhere strangled to death. This tramp should . . ."

Fargo had listened to enough. He swept up out of his crouch and slammed his right fist into Harvey's jaw. He didn't hold back. Harvey cried out and staggered but he didn't fall.

Fargo set himself and waded in but before he could land another blow Dugan and McNee leaped in, fists flying. Fargo blocked, countered, slipped punches but not all of them. Pain flared in his left cheek, his shoulder, his ribs. He got his left forearm up in time to deflect a looping swing by Dugan and retaliated with lightning jabs that drove Dugan back. McNee sprang in, and again Fargo's ribs complained. A quick hook, and Fargo had the satisfaction of pulping McNee's lower lip. For a moment he was clear but only for a moment. Harvey came at him again. Fargo stood his ground and gave as good as he got. He was so intent on Harvey that he forgot about Dugan and McNee but he was reminded when they flung themselves at his arms.

Fargo strained to break free. He had almost succeeded when Harvey hit him in the gut. He kicked Harvey in the shin and Harvey cocked his fists to hit him again. Succor came from an unexpected source.

"Here now, that's enough!" Tom Wilson cried, and shoved between them.

"Three against one. I won't have that."

"Out of my way, damn you," Harvey fumed. He tried to shove Wilson aside but Wilson held his ground.

"Simmer down, will you? The marshal's not going to like that you attacked this man."

"*He* took the first swing!" Harvey exploded, and grabbing Wilson by the shoulders, he pushed Wilson so hard that Wilson sprawled onto his back. There was a thud, and Wilson went limp.

"Tom?" one of the others said. The man rushed over and knelt. He slipped a hand under Wilson's head and drew it back, startled. His palm was smeared red. "Damn. He's bleeding. He hit his head on a rock."

"Is he alive?" asked another.

The man with the blood on his palm felt for a pulse and nodded. "He's just knocked out, is all."

Harvey whirled on Fargo. "It's your fault, you son of a bitch."

"You're the one who pushed him," Fargo said.

"Only because he was trying to defend you." Harvey drew his six-gun. "What do you say, boys? Why wait for the marshal? Let's make him tell us where Myrtle is."

"How do you propose we do that?" asked the man kneeling beside Tom Wilson.

"Easy as pie," Harvey said, and slashed the barrel of his revolver at Fargo's face.

It was called pistol-whipping. Lawmen would pistol-whip drunks and belligerents to subdue them. Sometimes the whipping was so severe that those who were beaten suffered a broken nose and busted teeth and were left black and blue for weeks.

Fargo had no intention of letting that happen. As Harvey swung, he ducked, and the pistol flashed over his head. Instantly he brought the heel of his right boot down on the tip of Dugan's left boot. Dugan howled in pain and his grip slackened enough that Fargo swung him bodily at McNee and both went tottering. Harvey was raising his arm to use the pistol. In a streak, Fargo had his Colt out and slammed the barrel against Harvey's face, splitting Harvey's cheek. Harvey forgot himself and clutched at his face; he would have done better to protect his gut.

Fargo drove his left fist in so far, he would swear his knuckles brushed Harvey's spine. Harvey buckled at the knees but Dugan and McNee had recovered and hurled themselves at Fargo, seeking to seize his arms as they had before. Fargo clipped Dugan across the head and Dugan toppled. McNee dodged, clawed for a pistol on his left hip, and was so slow unlimbering it that Fargo smashed him twice across the chin.

"Enough!" the man who was next to Tom Wilson cried. "In God's name, stop this!"

Fargo wanted to hit them some more. But both Dugan and McNee were down and Harvey was on his knees, doubled over. He nodded and stepped back.

Suddenly another townsman was behind him and jammed a cocked revolver against the back of his head.

"Hold it right there, mister."

"Danvers, what in hell are you doing?" asked the man kneeling beside Wilson.

"I think Harvey is right. If this hombre was innocent he wouldn't have made such a fuss." Danvers reached around and took Fargo's Colt. "Let go or I'll squeeze this trigger, so help me."

Fargo swore, and let go.

Harvey was struggling to his feet. "Thanks for seeing sense, Danvers," he said. "Now let's revive Dugan and McNee and get to it." He leveled his revolver at Fargo. "Fetch a rope."

Danvers moved toward their horses.

"What are you up to?" demanded the man on his knee. "It can't be what I think it is."

"Shut the hell up," Harvey said. "We're going to do what we should have done when we found this bastard." He grinned a vicious grin. "We're going to hang him."